Eight Years Till Sunlight

by

A. Abney

Contact

Email: aabney06@aol.com

Preface

Every day children are subjected to some form of abuse. A lot of these abuses go undetected for many years. Some are never known. This book is dedicated to the countless children who have endured the unimaginable horrors of abuse and neglect, their voices often silenced, their stories often untold. It's also to the survivors who have found the courage to speak their truth, to share their experiences, and to advocate for change. Their vulnerability in sharing their stories is a powerful act of defiance, a testament to their resilience, and an inspiration to those who have yet to find their voice. It is a testament to their quiet strength, their unwavering resilience, and their capacity for hope, even in the darkest of times. This is for every child who has suffered in silence, for every child

who has fought to survive, and for
every child who dreams of a future
free from fear and pain. Their
bravery inspires hope and fosters a
deeper understanding of the
profound and lasting impact of child
abuse, pushing us toward a future
where such horrors are a thing of the
past. It is to these courageous souls
that this book is most profoundly
dedicated.

Contents

Chapter 1: The Attic

The scent of freshly baked bread, usually a comforting aroma that filled their small kitchen, felt strangely muted this time. Five-year-old Joshua, perched on a stool, watched his mother knead the dough, her movements unusually jerky and her face etched with a fatigue he didn't understand. His father, a jovial man with a booming laugh and hands that always smelled of sawdust, was absent. The silence in his absence was a heavy blanket, smothering the usual cheerful chaos of their little home. His father's death, a sudden and unexplained heart attack, had cast a pall over everything, leaving behind a void that no amount of freshly baked bread could fill.

Joshua remembered the funeral, a blurry montage of somber faces and hushed whispers. He didn't fully grasp the concept of death, only the lingering sadness that clung to his mother like a shadow. She seemed different, quieter, her smiles less frequent, replaced by a pensive stillness that unnerved him. He missed his father's playful tickles, the bedtime stories, the feeling of secure warmth in his father's embrace. The world, once vibrant and filled with laughter, had lost its color.

The months after Joshua father's death were pretty solemn. He would look outside every day for his father's car to be gone like it usually is after he leaves for work, but it was still there. Every time he looked out that window there was the car, sitting as if it was waiting for it's master to return. Subconsciously Joshua didn't want to believe his father was gone, but with every passing day reality set in more and more. The reality of his father's death really started to set in when a strange man started coming by the house to see his mother.

Mr. Peterson's visits started out casual but became more frequent over the weeks. Mr. Peterson was very nice to Joshua and even started having a good relationship with him. Joshua could see that his mother was very fond of Mr. Peterson, maybe she just needed the attention after her husband's death.

One day while Joshua was playing, his mother sat him down for a talk. Joshua's mom told him that they would be moving out of state to live with Mr. Peterson. Mr. Peterson had gotten a promotion at his job and it required him to relocate to another state.

Within two weeks Joshua's mother had got everything packed up for the move to the new home.

The move to the new house was supposed to be a fresh start, a chance to rebuild their lives. It was a sprawling two-story colonial, bigger than their old cozy bungalow, nestled on a quiet street lined with identical houses, each one a miniature replica of the American dream. But the dream felt brittle, fragile, like an antique doll threatened to shatter at the slightest touch. The house felt cold despite its size, a chill that seeped from the walls and settled deep in Joshua's bones. The air itself hummed with an unseen tension, a low thrumming discord that resonated only in his young heart.

His mother, now dating Mr. Peterson, explained that the house was old and needed some work, a reason for the constant creaking of floorboards and the unsettling musty smell that emanated from the attic. Mr. Peterson, a tall, gaunt man with eyes that never quite met Joshua's, was quiet and reserved, a stark contrast to his father's boisterous personality. He had a way of making Joshua feel small and insignificant, a feeling that deepened with every passing day.

The house itself seemed to whisper secrets. There were shadows in the hallways that danced in the periphery of his vision, sounds in the dead of night that sent shivers down his spine. The attic, a place he was strictly forbidden from entering, became a symbol of mystery and fear, an unknown entity that lurked in the upper reaches of the house, its existence a palpable presence. He often heard muffled sounds emanating from the closed attic door

– the rustling of something, hushed whispers, occasional thuds. His childish imagination painted dark scenarios, monsters lurking in the darkness, but he was too afraid to voice his fear.

His mother's behavior underwent a subtle but disconcerting shift. Her affection, once overflowing, became measured, reserved, almost absent. She seemed preoccupied, her focus constantly elsewhere, her attention often diverted to Mr. Peterson. She wouldn't cuddle him at bedtime like before, and the bedtime stories, his cherished link to his father, ceased. The laughter in their home was replaced by a suffocating silence punctuated by tense exchanges between his mother and Mr. Peterson.

One evening, while playing in the yard, Joshua spotted Mr. Peterson heading toward the house carrying a large wooden chest. He watched as Mr. Peterson disappeared into the attic with the chest, the attic door creaking shut behind him with an ominous finality. The sound sent a shiver of fear through Joshua. He couldn't quite put his finger on it, but something felt wrong, profoundly, irrevocably wrong. The world, once a place of gentle familiarity, now felt alien and threatening, a space where shadows danced and secrets whispered.

The days that followed blurred into a disorienting montage of growing unease. His mother's smiles were fleeting, her touch less frequent. Meals became infrequent, portions smaller, the warmth of family suppers fading into a hunger that gnawed at his belly. His toys gathered dust in a corner, forgotten amidst the creeping unease. The comforting routine of his life, once predictable and reassuring, was unraveling, leaving behind a terrifying emptiness. The house, once a sanctuary, was transforming into a sinister prison, its walls closing in on him. He tried to tell his mother that he was scared, that something was wrong, but his words seemed to vanish into the pervasive silence of the house, swallowed by the unspoken tension between his mother and Mr. Peterson. His small voice, barely a whisper, was drowned out by the mounting sense of dread.

He began to notice inconsistencies, small discrepancies that heightened his fear. The friendly neighbor he used to see tending his garden, waving cheerfully, now seemed to avoid their house, her face etched with a strained, unreadable expression. The cheerful sounds of children playing on the street, once a background hum to his own playful days, became distant and faint, as if muted by an invisible wall. His world was shrinking, confining him to the increasingly suffocating interior of the house. He was beginning to sense that he was being deliberately isolated, his contact with the outside world dwindling to nothing more than occasional glimpses from the windows. The joy he once experienced, his youthful laughter, became a distant memory, echoing faintly within the growing cavern of fear.

The idyllic suburban setting, once a symbol of safety and security, transformed into a backdrop for a nightmare slowly unfolding. The normalcy of the neighborhood only served to amplify the horrors occurring behind closed doors, creating a stark and unnerving contrast between the perfect façade of the community and the decaying reality within their house. Joshua's innocence, his naivety, made him particularly vulnerable, his limited comprehension of the adult world leaving him adrift in a sea of suspicion and fear, unable to articulate or understand the gravity of the situation. His world was changing, irrevocably and terrifyingly. The day the world changed wasn't a single moment, but a slow, insidious creep of darkness, a subtle erosion of his once happy existence. The vibrant colors of his childhood faded into the grayscale of fear and confinement.

The attic door creaked shut, the sound swallowed by the silence that had become Joshua's constant companion. He pressed his small body against the cold, damp wood, his heart hammering against his ribs like a trapped bird. The darkness was immediate, a suffocating blanket that enveloped him, swallowing the last vestiges of light. He reached out, his fingers brushing against rough-hewn wood and layers of dust so thick it felt like a second skin. The air was thick with the smell of decay, a musty, acrid odor that clung to the back of his throat, choking him. This was different; this wasn't the playful exploration of a child venturing into a forbidden space. This was confinement.

He whimpered, a tiny sound lost in the vast emptiness of the attic. Tears welled in his eyes, hot and sticky on his cheeks. He called out for his mother, his voice a frail echo in the oppressive silence. "Mommy?" The word hung in the air, unanswered, swallowed by the oppressive quiet. The only response was the creak of the old house settling, a sound that seemed to mock his despair.

The attic was small, barely larger than a closet. A single, bare bulb hung precariously from the ceiling, its weak light barely piercing the gloom. The floorboards were uneven, rotting in places, and covered in a thick layer of dust. He stumbled, his small legs unsteady on the unstable ground. A cough wracked his small body, the dry air rasping in his lungs. He felt a sharp pain in his chest, a familiar ache that had begun to haunt him. The hunger, a constant companion, gnawed at his insides, a relentless ache that overshadowed everything else.

Days blurred into nights, each one indistinguishable from the last. Time became a meaningless concept, a blur of darkness punctuated by moments of gnawing hunger and suffocating loneliness. The only sounds were the creaks and groans of the old house, the occasional rustle of unseen creatures in the darkness, and the persistent, agonizing pangs of his empty stomach. He tried to sleep, curling into a ball in a corner, but the cold seeped into his bones, and the darkness pressed down on him, a heavy weight that stole his breath. His dreams were a jumble of fragmented memories, fleeting images of his father's smiling face, the warmth of his mother's embrace, all dissolving into the overwhelming reality of his desolate prison.

He found a small, cracked window high on the wall, a tiny portal to the outside world. He pressed his face against the cold glass, his breath fogging the surface. He watched the world go by, a silent observer, separated by an invisible wall of despair. He saw children playing in the street, their laughter a cruel mockery of his own silence. He saw cars driving by their occupants oblivious to his existence. He saw the sun rise and set, marking the passage of time, time he was losing, time that was slipping away like sand through his fingers.

The food, when it came, was meager—a stale piece of bread, a spoonful of watery soup, barely enough to sustain a bird, let alone a growing child. He ate slowly, savoring each bite, the hunger so intense it made his head spin. The physical discomfort was unrelenting; his body ached with hunger and cold, his skin dry and cracked. He was losing weight, his clothes hanging loosely on his frail frame. His reflection in the cracked windowpane was a stranger to him, a gaunt, pale figure that bore little resemblance to the cheerful child he once was.

One day, he heard a sound, a different sound, that broke the monotony of the silence. It was a sob, a muffled cry that sent a chill down his spine. It was his mother's voice, a sound he hadn't heard in what felt like an eternity. He scrambled to his feet, his heart pounding in his chest, hope flickering in the darkness. He crawled towards the attic door, his small hands clinging to the rough wood. The door creaked open, a sliver of light piercing the gloom. He saw his mother standing in the doorway, her face etched with sorrow, her eyes filled with a mixture of pain and guilt. She carried a bowl of thin broth.

She approached him slowly, her eyes avoiding his. She placed the bowl on the floor, her hand trembling. He looked at her, his small face a mixture of confusion and fear. He wanted to run to her, to feel the warmth of her embrace, but fear held him back. The hunger warred with the fear, and the fear always won. He looked down at the broth, his stomach churning with a mixture of hunger and nausea.

She said nothing, just watched him as he drank the thin liquid, every drop a testament to his desperate need. After he finished, she looked at him, her face filled with an anguished expression. She reached out her hand, but hesitated, then quickly withdrew it. She turned and left, closing the door behind her with a soft click. The click echoed the sound of his heart breaking, but this time he knew that it wasn't the hope of rescue but rather the acceptance of his grim reality. The confinement was no longer just physical but an entanglement of emotional and psychological deprivation. The silent scream locked within the walls of the attic seemed to amplify with each passing day, a silent symphony of despair. The sensory deprivation, the absence of human touch, and the unrelenting hunger were only the harsh realities of his newly constructed world.

The days continued in this pattern. His mother would appear occasionally, bringing him meager rations, her eyes filled with a mixture of guilt and something else, a chilling indifference that seemed to grow with each visit. She never spoke, never offered a word of comfort or explanation. The silence was as much a weapon of torture as the hunger and isolation. It was a silence that stole his voice, eroded his spirit, and left him hollowed out, an empty shell in a cramped, decaying attic. His once vibrant imagination faded, becoming the prisoner of his grim reality. The stories of his father, once a source of comfort, became distant whispers, fading echoes in the endless night.

The silence was broken only by his own sobs, the rustling of unseen creatures in the shadows, and the relentless gnawing of his hunger. He learned to live with the darkness, to navigate the cramped space in the pitch black. He discovered that the small window offered a view, not just of the outside world, but also of the moon and the stars. He began to count the stars, their distant light a flicker of hope in the infinite darkness that surrounded him. Counting the stars became his only connection to the world, his only escape from the suffocating reality of his imprisonment. His imagination, once a kaleidoscope of vibrant colors, slowly faded, replaced by a gray, monotonous landscape of hunger, fear, and despair. He learned to become invisible, to shrink into the shadows, so that his already faint presence would not disturb the unnerving silence. He was a ghost haunting the attic, his existence as fragile and imperceptible as the faint moonlight that illuminated his cramped, desolate prison. The attic was no longer just a space, but a testament to the darkness of human nature.

The counting of stars became a ritual, a desperate attempt to impose order on the chaos of his existence. Each star represented a moment, a breath, a sliver of hope in the vast emptiness. He'd assign names to them, weaving fantastical stories around their celestial positions, creating a universe of his own making to counter the bleak reality of his confinement. These celestial bodies became his friends, his silent companions in the desolate attic. He spoke to them, whispered his fears and hopes, pouring out his soul into the uncaring void of the night sky. It was a fragile shield against the encroaching despair, a testament to the enduring power of the human spirit to find solace even in the darkest of places.

But even the stars, once a beacon of hope, began to lose their luster. The subtle cruelty of his imprisonment was not merely physical; it was a slow, insidious erosion of his very being, a systematic dismantling of his spirit. The lack of human interaction, the absence of warmth and affection, began to take its toll. His mother's sporadic visits, once a glimmer of hope, now served as a stark reminder of her betrayal. Her silence, her averted gaze, spoke volumes more than any scream or outburst ever could.

The meager rations became less frequent. The occasional bowl of thin broth transformed into a single, stale piece of bread every other day, leaving him perpetually hungry. His body became a testament to deprivation. The skeletal frame barely held together by his already stretched skin. His bones pressed against his paper-thin skin, every movement and agony. The constant hunger was a relentless physical torment that gnawed at his insides, a constant reminder of his powerlessness. His frail body echoed his broken spirit. He lost track of time, days bleeding into weeks, weeks into months, months into years. The concept of time itself began to distort, a fluid entity that held no meaning within the confines of his prison.

The psychological manipulation was more subtle, more insidious. His captors didn't need to inflict physical violence. The silence, the neglect, the occasional fleeting moment of cold indifference from his mother were enough to chip away at his self-worth, to erode his hope. He began to question his own existence, his own worth. Was he even worthy of love? Was he even worth saving? The insidious whispers of self-doubt crept into his mind, planting seeds of despair that took root and grew into monstrous vines of self-loathing.

He started to lose his sense of identity. The vibrant, energetic child he once was became a faint memory, a ghost haunting the edges of his consciousness. He was becoming invisible, both to himself and to the world outside. He ceased to exist as a person, he began to exist as a shadow. He became a silent observer of his own slow disintegration. He no longer even fought for survival. He merely persisted.

But the human spirit is resilient. Even as his hope dwindled, a spark remained. It wasn't a conscious decision, a defiant act of will, but rather a subconscious survival mechanism. In the dead of night, when the darkness was at its most profound, when his hunger was at its most acute, he would retreat into a world of fantasy. He would create elaborate stories, populate them with fantastical characters, and immerse himself in these imaginary realms. He would escape the confines of the attic, soaring through the stars on the backs of magical creatures. He became a knight, a warrior, a hero battling dragons and rescuing princesses. He was the master of his own destiny, a powerful figure in a world where he was completely powerless.

These fantastical tales were more than just an escape; they were a lifeline, a way to maintain a sense of self, a way to keep the flicker of hope alive. He built intricate castles in the air, populated by imaginary friends who loved and cherished him. These fantasies were not simply escapism; they were an act of defiance, a refusal to surrender to the darkness that threatened to consume him.

His creativity became his sanctuary. He used the limited resources at his disposal, drawing pictures in the dust with his finger, crafting miniature objects from scraps of wood and cloth. He created a world of art and imagination. The dust-covered floor became a canvas, the rough-hewn wood his sculpting tools. These creations were acts of self-expression, a way to assert his individuality in a world that had tried to erase him.

Yet, the line between reality and fantasy began to blur. The stark reality of his imprisonment became increasingly intertwined with the vibrant images of his imagination. He would sometimes find himself calling out to his imaginary friends, only to be met with the oppressive silence of the attic. The fantasy world, once a refuge, now became a source of confusion and despair. He began to question which world was real, which world was the illusion. The boundaries between his dreams and reality dissolved in the suffocating confinement of his prison.

The years wore on, leaving an indelible mark on his young mind and body. The physical deprivation was matched by the slow, relentless erosion of his hope. The once bright flame of childhood dreams had been reduced to a flickering ember, threatened at any moment by the encroaching darkness. Yet, the ember persisted, fueled by the indomitable spirit of a child who had endured more than any child ever should. The survival instinct, a powerful force driving him through the unrelenting bleakness, was the only beacon of hope that prevented his total demise, a constant reminder of the tenacious hold of the human will to survive even amidst the most catastrophic circumstances. The attic became not just a prison, but a crucible, testing his strength, his spirit, and his capacity for enduring unimaginable hardship. His small form, ravaged by hunger and isolation, held within it a resilience that would eventually carry him towards a hard-fought freedom.

The dust motes dancing in the single shaft of sunlight that pierced the attic's gloom were sometimes joined by other, more fleeting visitors. A tiny sparrow, braver than most, would occasionally perch on the windowsill, its chirping a fragile melody against the oppressive silence. Joshua would watch it, mesmerized, imagining himself soaring alongside it, free from the confines of his prison. He'd whisper stories to the bird, confiding his deepest fears and unspoken hopes, finding solace in its fleeting presence. It was a small act of grace, a momentary connection to the living world outside, a reminder that life, in all its vibrant forms, still existed.

One particularly harsh winter, a gust of wind rattled the attic window, carrying with it the faint scent of woodsmoke and something sweeter, something like gingerbread. The aroma, faint yet unmistakable, lingered for a few precious moments before being swallowed by the stale air of the attic. It was a fleeting sensory experience, yet it sparked a cascade of memories, a rush of images from a life that felt distant, almost mythical. The scent of gingerbread conjured memories of Christmases past, of warmth and laughter, of a family gathered around a crackling fire, a stark contrast to the cold, empty space he inhabited. The memory, though bittersweet, was a life raft in the sea of despair, offering a brief respite from the crushing weight of his isolation.

Another time, he heard a child's laughter carried on the wind. It was muffled and distant, yet distinct enough to pierce the thick walls of his self-imposed silence. He strained his ears, trying to pinpoint its source, clinging to the sound as if it were a lifeline. The laughter, echoing faintly from somewhere in the distance, painted a vibrant picture of a world he had left behind, a world of carefree joy and innocent abandon. It was a fleeting moment, a whispered promise of a life that could still exist, a life that he might one day reclaim. He clutched the memory close, a precious jewel in the darkness.

There were nights when the moon shone particularly bright, casting long, ethereal shadows across the attic floor. On those nights, the stars seemed closer, their light less distant, their silent vigil a source of quiet comfort. He'd lie on the floor, staring up at the celestial tapestry, and imagine that the stars were whispering stories, their light a silent reassurance that he was not forgotten. It was in these moments of quiet contemplation that he found the strength to carry on, to endure the unbearable weight of his isolation. He would weave these moments into the fantastical narratives of his imagination, using the celestial bodies as actors in his private dramas, each star a unique character in his ongoing saga of survival.

He even developed a unique relationship with the rats that occasionally ventured into his domain. At first, he feared them, these creatures of the shadows that shared his prison. But over time, he began to observe them, recognizing their own tenacity, their own struggle for survival. He started leaving small portions of his meager rations for them, a silent truce in the desolate battleground of the attic. He even began to assign names to them, weaving them into his fantastical narratives, transforming them from creatures of fear into companions in his solitary existence. It was a strange form of connection, a fragile bond formed in the midst of despair, yet it was another small act of grace, a testament to the enduring power of hope.

Once, he heard a faint melody drifting up from the house below. It was a simple tune, played on a piano, and it sounded like a lullaby. The music, though faint and distant, filled the attic with a sense of unexpected peace. It was a brief respite from the oppressive silence, a fleeting moment of beauty and calm in the midst of unrelenting darkness.

The music transported him to a place of tranquility, a temporary escape from the harsh reality of his confinement. He closed his eyes, imagining the musician, his fingers dancing across the keys, creating a haven of sound.

Sometimes, when the moon was particularly bright, he could make out the shapes of the trees outside his window. He would spend hours watching them sway in the breeze, their silent movement a calming rhythm in the monotonous stillness of the attic. He'd imagine himself climbing them, reaching for the branches, feeling the rough bark against his skin. It was an escape, a chance to explore the world he was forbidden to enter, a world alive with life, color and energy, a world so different from his own bleak reality. He would weave these trees into his fantastical stories, transforming them into enchanted forests, each branch holding secrets, each leaf a whispered promise.

The attic was a prison, a crucible of despair, but even within its confines, moments of grace, however fleeting, found their way in. A sparrow's song, the scent of gingerbread, a child's laughter, moonlight filtering through the cracks in the walls, a simple melody played on a distant piano, the silent dance of trees swaying in the breeze - these were the ephemeral sparks that illuminated the long nights, sustaining his spirit, preventing the encroaching darkness from completely extinguishing the flame of hope within him. They were the tiny threads of connection to the world, weaving a subtle tapestry of hope against the stark reality of his confinement. They were a silent testament to the resilience of the human spirit, even in the face of unimaginable hardship. They were moments of grace, and they were everything. They were the quiet whispers that kept his spirit alive, reminding him that even in the darkest corners of the world, there is always a sliver of light. And that sliver of light, he knew, was worth fighting for. He held onto them like precious jewels, cherishing them, nurturing them, allowing them to fuel the ember of hope within his young heart, keeping it burning against all odds. They were his solace, his comfort, his promise. They were his moments of grace, his silent companions in the long, dark years of his confinement. And they were the reason he survived.

The rhythmic dripping of water from a leaky pipe became his metronome, marking the passage of time in the otherwise silent attic. He counted the drops, each one a tiny tick on the clock of his captivity, a way to measure the relentless march of days and nights. He developed a complex system of counting, assigning different values to the drips, creating a numerical tapestry that stretched across the years. This was his own unique calendar, a way to maintain a sense of order in the chaotic landscape of his imprisonment. It was a small act of control, a subtle defiance against the randomness of his existence. It wasn't just counting; it was a way of marking his continued existence, a defiant affirmation of his presence in the world.

He learned to read the subtle changes in the attic's environment as indicators of the outside world. A shift in wind direction might bring a different scent, a hint of the distant city, of life beyond his walls. The intensity of the sunlight filtering through the single grimy windowpane altered with the seasons, providing a crude but reliable marker of the passage of the year. He observed the shadows cast by the sun, noting their gradual shift as the days lengthened and shortened, silently tracking the progression of time. The faint sounds from the house below – the creaks of the floorboards, the hum of the refrigerator, the occasional clash of pans – became a muted symphony that he learned to interpret. It was his own way of decoding the world beyond, a silent conversation with a world he was excluded from. The changes were subtle, almost imperceptible to most, but to Joshua, they were crucial clues, threads leading to a reality just out of reach.

His imagination became his sanctuary, a place where he could escape the harsh reality of his confinement. He created elaborate worlds in his mind, populated by fantastical creatures and daring adventurers. He was the hero of his own stories, a brave knight rescuing damsels in distress, a fearless explorer charting uncharted territories, a powerful wizard wielding magic to overcome insurmountable odds. He spun yarns that entwined the few real-world elements within the attic with impossible feats of heroism and wonder. The leaky pipe became a magical fountain, the rats his loyal companions, the dust motes sparkling fairies. The single window was the gateway to an endless, vibrant world, the trees outside its frame transformed into enchanted forests teeming with life.

These fantastical narratives were not mere escapes; they were survival mechanisms. They provided comfort, purpose, and a sense of control in a world where he had none. His imagination was a shield against despair, a constant source of hope and resilience. He created intricate storylines, building characters, crafting dialogues, and resolving conflicts. This wasn't passive daydreaming; it was the deliberate creation of a complex, multifaceted world, a testament to his resilience and creativity. The stories were a reflection of his desperate need for meaning, for connection, for agency. They were his way of fighting back against the encroaching darkness, of reclaiming a sense of self. He poured his emotional energy into these imagined realities, using them as a way to process his trauma, to find solace and strength. The details, painstakingly crafted and revisited, became a means of creating order within chaos.

He clung to fragmented memories of his life before the attic, precious scraps of a past he desperately tried to retain. The scent of his father's pipe tobacco, the feel of his mother's hand in his, the taste of his grandmother's apple pie – these fleeting sensory experiences became anchors in the sea of his isolation. He would recall these sensory details with agonizing clarity, each one a tiny spark illuminating the darkness of his present. He nurtured these memories, replaying them again and again in his mind, holding onto them as if they were life rafts in a storm-tossed sea. These were the remnants of a life he had lost, a world he was determined not to forget. He refused to let his memories fade, cherishing them as a reminder of who he was before, a reminder of the life he was fighting to reclaim. They were a tangible link to a past that provided him with a sense of identity, a sense of self.

He developed subtle acts of resistance, tiny rebellions against his captors. He wouldn't cooperate fully, holding onto a quiet sense of defiance that ran beneath the surface of his outward compliance. He would intentionally misplace things, creating a tiny amount of inconvenience. This wasn't an overtly hostile act but a small, simmering rebellion played out in the details. He would subtly rearrange objects in the attic, a silent act of asserting his presence, a silent declaration of "I am here." He learned to interpret his captors' routines, anticipating their movements, recognizing patterns in their behavior, creating a silent game of cat and mouse. This subtle resistance was a way of maintaining a sense of agency, a way of retaining his own will. It might have seemed insignificant to an outsider, but to Joshua, it was a crucial act of survival.

His physical resilience was another component of his survival. The limited food supply forced him to conserve his energy, to move deliberately, strategically. He developed an almost animalistic awareness of his body, carefully rationing his movements to conserve strength. This wasn't just physical; it was mental, a conscious effort to regulate his responses, manage his resources, and survive. His body became an instrument of survival, responding to the demands of his environment, learning to function on minimal resources. The physical hardship he endured forged a resilient spirit, a powerful determination to not simply survive, but to endure.

In the end, it wasn't any single act but the accumulation of these small acts of coping, these tiny triumphs of the human spirit, that allowed Joshua to survive. The counting of water drops, the weaving of fantastical stories, the retention of precious memories, the subtle acts of defiance – these were the threads that wove together the tapestry of his survival. They were the quiet acts of resilience that kept hope alive, fueling the ember that refused to be extinguished, and ultimately, they were the seeds of his survival, the building blocks upon which he would rebuild his life. They were the silent testaments to the indomitable strength of the human spirit, even in the face of unimaginable hardship. They were the quiet, persistent acts of self-preservation that allowed him to endure. They were the reasons he survived. And they were his story.

Days turned to weeks, and weeks turned to months until time no longer mattered. For Joshua it was just one continuous day. A bad dream that he hoped to wake up from soon.

Chapter 2: The Fire

The first crackle was like a whisper, a tiny intrusion on the usual silence of the attic. It wasn't the rhythmic drip of the leaky pipe, nor the familiar creak of the floorboards below. It was something new, something sharp and insistent, a sound that pricked at the edges of his carefully constructed world. At first, he dismissed it, attributing it to a particularly boisterous rat or the settling of the old timbers. But the whispers grew, coalescing into a low hum that vibrated through the floorboards, a primal tremor in the bones of the house. Then came the smell – acrid, sharp, stinging his nostrils with a terrifying familiarity. Smoke.

Panic, a cold, clammy hand, squeezed his chest. He scrambled to his feet, his emaciated frame trembling, his heart pounding a frantic rhythm against his ribs. He stumbled towards the single grimy window, his eyes straining to pierce the gathering darkness. He saw it then, a flicker of orange in the distance, a malevolent eye staring back at him from the inky night. It wasn't a star, it wasn't the moon; it was something far more terrifying. It was fire.

The flickering light grew, painting the attic walls in a grotesque, shifting display of orange and black. The hum intensified, transforming into a guttural roar that seemed to shake the very foundations of the house. The air grew thick, heavy with the choking scent of burning wood and melting plastic. Each breath seared his lungs, filling his mouth with the bitter taste of smoke. He coughed, a dry, rattling cough that racked his frail body. His eyes watered, blurring the already indistinct shapes of the attic.

The floorboards beneath his feet began to tremble violently, the rhythmic groaning of the house intensifying into a cacophony of cracking and splintering wood. He felt a surge of heat, a wave of searing air that washed over him, pushing him back against the cold stone wall. He pressed himself against the wall, his body trembling, his senses overwhelmed by the growing inferno. The air grew hotter, the smoke thicker, making it almost impossible to breathe. He clawed at the dusty windowpane, his fingernails scraping against the glass, a desperate attempt to find a way out, a desperate attempt to escape the suffocating heat and the poisonous smoke.

The flames, now licking the edges of the attic, danced and writhed like malevolent spirits, their fiery tongues reaching out to devour everything in their path. He could hear the crackling and popping of the fire, a relentless symphony of destruction. He could feel the heat radiating from the floor, searing his skin, burning his lungs. He could smell the burning wood, the acrid stench of smoke, the terrifying smell of his impending doom. The attic, his prison for so many years, was transforming into a furnace, a blazing inferno that threatened to consume him.

He moved instinctively, his body reacting without the direction of his mind, his fight-or-flight response finally kicking in. He scrambled over the debris that littered the attic floor, his hands and knees scraping against the rough wood. The

shadows of the flames danced and
stretched, casting long, grotesque
figures that twisted and writhed
before him, his old protectors and
comforts – the familiar darkness of
the attic and his imagination now
monstrous figures. He bumped into
the pile of forgotten toys, their once
colorful paints now scorched and
blackened. He stumbled over the old
trunk where he kept his meager
possessions, his cherished
memories, now turned to ash and
embers. His careful structure of
memory was collapsing around him.

The heat was unbearable. The smoke
was choking him. His lungs burned,
each breath a torturous act of
defiance. He could feel the flames
getting closer, the searing heat
pressing against his skin,
threatening to consume him. He
knew he had to escape, but escape
seemed impossible. The only way

out was blocked by the raging inferno. He was trapped.

Then, through the haze of smoke and the agonizing pain, he heard it – the distant sound of sirens, a rising crescendo that cut through the roar of the flames. Hope, a fragile ember, flickered in his heart. He pushed himself to his feet, his legs shaky, his body weak, but his determination unwavering. He scrambled towards the attic door, his hands outstretched, searching for the doorknob, desperate to find salvation.

The door was jammed, the wood warped and swollen by the intense heat. He pulled and pushed, his feeble strength pitted against the unforgiving power of the flames. He felt the scorching heat pressing against his face, his skin burning, his lungs screaming for air. He pulled again, and again, his mind focused on the distant sirens, his body driven by a fierce will to survive. The door gave way with a groan of tortured wood.

He stumbled out of the attic, into the swirling chaos of smoke and flames. The intense heat hit him like a wall, a physical manifestation of the terror he felt, but the sound of the sirens was louder now, a beacon of hope guiding him through the inferno. He staggered forward, his body weak, his vision blurred, but driven by the desperate need to live, to finally escape the prison of his eight-year confinement. He stumbled through the flames, feeling the scorching heat consuming him, but his heart pounded with hope as he moved closer towards the sounds of salvation. He could taste the hope, the acrid and sweet taste of a new beginning. The fire had been the trigger, the catalyst for his escape, the blazing inferno his unexpected salvation. The flames that had threatened to consume him had instead set him free.

The roar of the flames was deafening, a monstrous symphony of destruction that dwarfed even the frantic pounding of his own heart. He stumbled blindly through the smoke-filled hallway, his lungs burning, his vision blurred. The heat was unbearable, a searing wave that washed over him, threatening to consume him entirely. Yet, he pressed on, driven by an instinct for survival that had lain dormant for eight long years, now awakened by the terrifying embrace of the fire.

Then, through the swirling haze of smoke and the agonizing pain, he saw them. Figures, silhouetted against the orange glow of the inferno, moving with a purpose that seemed both alien and strangely

comforting. Firefighters, their faces
obscured by masks, their
movements precise and efficient,
battling the raging fire with a calm
determination that contrasted
sharply with the chaos around him.
They were not the monstrous figures
of his imagination; they were his
rescuers.

One of them spotted him, a fleeting
glimpse through the smoke-filled
air. He saw a figure pause, then
move towards him with surprising
speed, seemingly materializing out
of the smoke like a phantom. The
firefighter reached him, kneeling
beside him, his movements gentle
despite the urgent situation. He felt
a strong arm wrap around him,
lifting him, carrying him away from
the inferno. The world became a
blur of motion, a kaleidoscope of
colors and sounds, a dizzying
transition from the stifling darkness

of the attic to the chaotic brilliance of the fire.

The air outside was cool and crisp, a stark contrast to the suffocating heat of the burning house. He lay on the grass, his body trembling, his lungs heaving, the world spinning around him. He tasted the cool night air, an alien sensation that sent a shiver down his spine. The faces above him swam into focus. More firefighters, their helmets gleaming under the emergency lights, their eyes filled with a mixture of shock and concern. He heard voices, a cacophony of sounds – shouts, sirens, the crackle of the fire – but none of it penetrated the numb fog that enveloped his mind.

He was conscious of hands, gentle yet firm, attending to him. He felt the rough texture of a blanket draped over him, a welcome respite from the cold. Then came the sirens

– a deafening chorus of emergency
vehicles that intensified with each
passing moment. He saw the flash of
cameras, the bright glow of flashing
lights, a stark visual representation
of the world he had been cut off
from for so long. The world was
overwhelming, a violent rush of
sensations after years of deprivation.
It was a world he barely recognized.

The paramedics arrived quickly,
their movements swift and
professional. They examined him,
their touch careful, their faces
serious. He could feel their scrutiny,
a silent assessment of his frail body.
He weighed a mere ninety pounds, a
skeletal figure barely clinging to life.
His skin was paper-thin, stretched
taut over bone, marred by scars and
bruises, testament to years of neglect
and abuse. His hair was matted and
dirty, his eyes wide and hollow,

reflecting the haunting emptiness of his past.

The journey to the hospital was a blur. He remembered the flashing lights, the sirens, the rush of the ambulance. He remembered the sensation of being wrapped in a warm blanket, the cool touch of an IV needle in his arm. He drifted in and out of consciousness, his mind overwhelmed by the intensity of his new reality. The stark contrasts between the deprivation and isolation of the attic and the sudden influx of activity and attention were almost too much to bear.

In the sterile environment of the hospital room, the reality of his situation began to settle. The doctors and nurses examined him with a mixture of concern and disbelief. Their faces were solemn, their movements careful as they ran tests and monitored his vital signs. He overheard hushed conversations, words like "malnutrition," "dehydration," and "severe neglect" whispered in low tones. He understood these terms not from their clinical definitions, but from the visceral memory of hunger, thirst, and the crushing weight of loneliness. These were the sensations that had defined his existence for the past eight years, now codified into clinical terms.

News of his rescue spread quickly. The story of the boy found in the attic of a burning house, emaciated and near death, captivated the media. Reporters and photographers descended upon the hospital, their presence a jarring reminder of the world outside, a world he was now struggling to understand. He learned about the fire, about the bravery of the firefighters who had saved him, about the outpouring of support from the community. The events felt surreal, a dream from which he might wake up back in his dark, suffocating prison.

The initial shock and disbelief gave way to a cautious optimism as he began his recovery. The physical healing was slow and arduous, a painstaking process of regaining strength and nourishment. But it was the emotional healing that proved to be the most challenging. The years of isolation, the trauma of neglect and abuse, left deep scars on his psyche. He began to grapple with the profound psychological impact of his ordeal, the years spent in the dark shadows of the attic. He grappled with trust, connection, and the overwhelming knowledge of his past.

The discovery of Joshua ignited a firestorm of outrage and public scrutiny. The authorities launched a full-scale investigation into the events leading up to his rescue. The investigation led to the arrest and subsequent conviction of his mother and her boyfriend on multiple counts of child abuse and neglect. The legal battle was long and arduous, but ultimately, justice was served. His mother and her boyfriend were brought to justice, their actions condemned not only by the court but by the wider community.

Joshua's rescue was not just a physical liberation; it was also a symbol of the vulnerability of children, the failures of the system designed to protect them, and the profound resilience of the human spirit. It was a story of survival against impossible odds. His rescue marked the start of a long and difficult journey toward healing, a journey that would require courage,

patience, and unwavering support.
He was, finally, free. The fire that
had threatened to consume him had
instead become the instrument of his
liberation. The rescue was the first
step on his arduous path to healing,
a long journey filled with both the
pain of facing the past and the hope
of building a future he'd never had
before. The embers of trauma still
smoldered, yet a flicker of hope
ignited, casting a hopeful light on
the horizon of his new life.

The world outside was a cacophony.
The sirens, a relentless, wailing
chorus that had initially seemed a
terrifying assault, now faded into a
dull hum in the background. The
sharp, clean scent of antiseptic in the
hospital room, a stark contrast to the
musty, stale air of the attic, initially
felt alien, then strangely comforting.
The soft, white sheets, cool against
his skin, were a luxury he hadn't

known existed. He lay there, a fragile vessel clinging to the edge of consciousness, the world a kaleidoscope of unfamiliar sensations.

His eyes, accustomed to the perpetual gloom of the attic, struggled to adjust to the bright fluorescent lights. Every flicker, every shadow, sent a jolt of apprehension through his body. The soft murmurs of the nurses, the rhythmic beeping of machines, the gentle rustle of sheets – sounds he had never experienced before – filled him with both curiosity and a deep-seated unease. The simple act of breathing felt different; the air, clean and unburdened by the smoke and dust of the fire, filled his lungs with a surprising lightness.

The first few days were a blur of tests, examinations, and intravenous drips. He endured countless pokes and prods, the invasive procedures triggering a wave of fear and distrust. The hands that touched him, though meant to heal, initially felt like an invasion, a violation of the fragile sanctuary he'd built around himself in the attic. His skeletal frame, barely clinging to life, was a testament to years of deprivation. The doctors talked amongst themselves, their words veiled in medical jargon that meant little to him. He caught glimpses of their expressions - a mixture of pity, disbelief, and professional detachment.

Slowly, painstakingly, his body began to heal. The IV fluids replenished the vital fluids drained from his body. The nutrient-rich food, something he'd only ever dreamed of, gradually restored some of his lost weight. Yet, the physical healing was a slow, agonizing process. Every bite was a struggle, every movement and effort. His muscles, atrophied from years of disuse, ached and protested with every attempt at exertion. The scars on his body, a grotesque map of his past suffering, remained as a constant reminder of his ordeal.

His initial encounters with the outside world were jarring. The sheer volume of sights, sounds, and smells was overwhelming. The vibrant colors of the city, the constant stream of people, the relentless hum of traffic – these were sensations that were foreign and, at times, terrifying. He retreated into himself, his eyes downcast, his body tense. The world felt vast and intimidating because it had been eight long years since he last seen or felt the outdoors.

But amidst the fear and confusion, there were glimmers of hope. The kindness of the nurses, the gentle touch of a doctor, the soft murmur of reassuring words – these small acts of compassion chipped away at the walls he had erected around his heart. He found solace in the quiet moments, in the simple act of watching the sun rise through the hospital window. The rising sun, a symbol of hope and a promise of a new dawn.

The media attention, however, felt like an intrusion. The flashing lights, the incessant questions from reporters, the intrusive stares of photographers – it all added to the sense of unease and vulnerability. He became increasingly withdrawn, his face a mask of impassivity. He felt as though he was on display, a specimen under the microscope of public scrutiny. His privacy was invaded. The weight of the world felt immense.

But alongside the intrusion came the messages of support. Cards, letters, and gifts arrived daily, sent from people across the country. These were messages of hope and encouragement, offering him strength and comfort. The kindness of strangers was unexpected, a balm to his wounded spirit. It was as if the entire world was reaching out to him.

His rescue, though undeniably traumatic, marked the start of a profound journey of healing. The physical scars would remain, but the emotional wounds ran deeper. The years of isolation had left him profoundly scarred, creating a chasm of distrust and alienation between him and the world. The path towards healing would be long and complex, requiring courage, patience, and unwavering support.

As the weeks turned into months, Joshua started to engage with the world around him in small ways. He began to interact with the other children at the hospital, sharing hesitant smiles and tentative conversations. He started participating in simple activities, such as coloring and reading. He watched animated movies and cartoons, finding joy in these simple pleasures. He rediscovered laughter, a sound that had been absent for too long. It wasn't easy, and there were times when the memories of the attic crept back into his thoughts, plunging him into the darkness of his past.

The initial awe and fear gave way to a cautious curiosity about this new world. He learned about things that were fundamental to most children, simple yet amazing concepts. He learned about the joy of playing, exploring, and interacting with others. He started attending therapy, working through the trauma with a kind and compassionate counselor who helped him navigate his emotions and confront his past.

The journey was arduous, but Joshua's resilience proved remarkable. He was a survivor, a testament to the strength of the human spirit. He faced every challenge with a quiet determination, a fierce will to reclaim his life. His spirit was unbroken. The fire had not only rescued him from his prison, but also ignited a flame of hope within him. He was free, not just from the confines of the attic, but from the shackles of fear and despair. The future stretched before him, daunting yet full of possibilities. He clung to the hope of a future worth living. He was a boy who had known only darkness, but now, he was beginning to see the light. The fire had destroyed his past, but it had also created the possibility of a new beginning. He was ready to embrace the challenges and difficulties, understanding the journey ahead would be long and winding. He was ready to begin.

The acrid smell of smoke still clung to the air, even days after the fire had been extinguished. The charred remains of the house stood as a stark monument to the horrors it had concealed. Amidst the debris, investigators sifted through the ashes, their faces grim, their movements methodical. The scene was a grim tableau of devastation, a testament to the inferno that had consumed the building. But more importantly, it was a crime scene, the starting point of an investigation that would uncover a story far more sinister than the blaze itself.

Detective Rosewood, a seasoned veteran with a weary gaze and a heart hardened by years on the force, surveyed the scene. He'd seen his share of fires, but this one felt different. There was a palpable sense of unease, a chilling silence that hung heavy in the air. It wasn't just the destruction; it was the inexplicable absence of anyone else within the burned structure, besides the already hospitalized young boy.

The initial reports had been confusing. A small fire, quickly extinguished by the neighborhood's swift response. A woman and her boyfriend, slightly injured, taken to the hospital. And then, the discovery. A boy, emaciated, hidden away in the attic, his existence unknown to everyone but his captors. A boy, rescued from a living hell.

The investigation moved swiftly. The fire marshal's report confirmed the fire was accidental, likely sparked by a carelessly discarded cigarette. But that wasn't the focus. The focus was on the conditions under which Joshua had lived – the years of neglect, abuse, and confinement. The attic, now a skeletal frame, had been his prison for eight long years. Photographs taken during the initial rescue circulated silently among the investigators, a stark reminder of the horror they were dealing with. The boy's skeletal frame, his vacant eyes, the silent screams etched on his face. The pictures were haunting.

The arrest of Joshua's mother, Sarah, and her boyfriend, Mark, followed quickly. They had been questioned at the hospital, their initial denials crumbling under the weight of evidence. The physical evidence was damning. The condition of the attic, the lack of food and necessities, the clear signs of neglect and abuse – it all painted a horrifying picture of their cruelty. And when confronted with Joshua's testimony, however fragmented and traumatized, their facade of normalcy shattered completely. Their arrests were met with a collective gasp of outrage in the community, and a wave of relief for the now-safe boy.

The legal proceedings were meticulous and thorough. Sarah and Mark were charged with multiple counts of child abuse, kidnapping, and neglect. The prosecution's case was overwhelmingly strong, fueled by overwhelming evidence and testimonies from the hospital staff who cared for the severely malnourished and traumatized boy.

Their lawyers fought hard, attempting to paint a picture of negligence rather than malicious intent. They argued they were overburdened, struggling financially, and simply didn't know how to care for a child. But their arguments fell on deaf ears, their pleas rejected by a jury who had witnessed the horrific evidence firsthand.

The media frenzy that followed was intense. The story of Joshua, the boy rescued from the attic, captured the nation's attention. His ordeal became a symbol of the vulnerabilities within the child protection system, a stark reminder of the horrors that can occur behind closed doors. The newspapers, television channels, and online platforms were filled with Joshua's story, alongside editorials questioning the efficacy of social services and the failures of the system that had allowed such a tragedy to unfold. The media coverage was relentless, a double-edged sword that brought attention to the issue but also invaded Joshua's fragile privacy. The initial outpouring of support was profound, but the subsequent sensationalism began to wear on him and the people caring for him.

The local Child Protective Services (CPS) came under intense scrutiny. Questions were raised about why Joshua's plight had gone unnoticed for so long. Were there missed opportunities? Had red flags been ignored? The investigation into CPS extended beyond the immediate case, leading to significant internal reviews and reforms to improve their investigative processes and procedures. The incident served as a wake-up call, forcing a thorough examination of the systems designed to protect vulnerable children.

Beyond the legal battles and media attention, there was the immense task of rebuilding Joshua's life. The physical rehabilitation was just the beginning. He faced years of therapy, grappling with the psychological trauma inflicted upon him. The process was slow, agonizing, and fraught with setbacks. The scars, both physical and emotional, were profound and pervasive.

His journey through the foster care system was fraught with challenges. He initially struggled to trust adults, to form bonds, to believe in kindness. His emotional landscape was a minefield of fear and mistrust. Every hand outstretched felt like a potential threat, every act of kindness a potential trap. His therapist worked tirelessly, guiding him through the maze of his memories, helping him to understand and process the trauma, to begin to rebuild his shattered sense of self. He learned to differentiate between genuine affection and malicious intent, a delicate process demanding patience and unwavering support.

The support network surrounding Joshua grew. Social workers, therapists, teachers, and volunteers worked tirelessly to provide him with the love, care, and guidance he needed. The outpouring of support from the community continued, transforming from media sensation to genuine concern and empathy. He found solace in the simple acts of kindness, in the warm smiles and reassuring words. The volunteers were there to support him in all his endeavors, assisting him in rebuilding trust in the world around him.

He learned to ride a bicycle, his laughter echoing through the park, a sound that had been absent for far too long. He learned to play, to engage with other children, slowly, tentatively, letting down his guard, discovering the joy of friendship. He started school, struggling at first, but determined to learn, to catch up, to prove to himself that he could overcome the obstacles that life had thrown his way. The journey was arduous, filled with tears and frustrations, but the glimmers of hope that emerged were bright and unwavering.

The aftermath of the fire was not simply the physical cleanup, the legal battles, or the media circus; it was the slow, painstaking process of healing. It was a testament to the resilience of the human spirit, the

unwavering strength of a boy who
had endured the unthinkable.
Joshua's story became a symbol of
hope, a reminder that even in the
darkest of circumstances, there can
be light. And that light, flickering at
first, grew stronger with every day,
every step, every milestone along his
path towards healing. The fire had
been a catalyst, the crucible through
which his resilience was forged and
his spirit was tempered. He was a
survivor. He was a testament to the
enduring strength of the human
will, and a beacon of hope to others
who had suffered in silence. He was
ready to face his future. He was
ready to live.

The sterile smell of antiseptic and
the faint whiff of disinfectant did
little to mask the underlying scent of
fear that clung to Joshua like a
second skin. He lay in the hospital
bed, a pale, frail figure wrapped in a

too-large hospital gown, his eyes
wide and unfocused. The fire, the
chaos, the sudden intrusion into his
eight-year prison – it all felt like a
disorienting nightmare, a surreal
break from the long, monotonous
routine of confinement.

His rescue felt less like liberation
and more like a forced ejection into a
world he didn't understand. The
faces that surrounded him – doctors,
nurses, social workers – were a blur
of concern, their words a jumble of
unfamiliar terms and well-meaning
platitudes that held little meaning to
him. The world outside the attic was
a cacophony of sights and sounds,
overwhelming his senses and
triggering a surge of anxiety that
tightened its icy grip around his
chest. He flinched at sudden noises,
recoiled from unexpected touches,
and retreated into himself, a

frightened animal cornered in a strange, unfamiliar cage.

His initial placement in foster care was…tentative. He was assigned to a foster family, the Millers, a seemingly kind couple with two teenage children who, despite their initial hesitation, seemed determined to help him adjust. Mrs. Miller, a soft-spoken woman with warm eyes, approached him cautiously, offering a gentle smile and a quiet word. Mr. Miller, a burly man with a quiet demeanor, maintained a respectful distance, allowing Joshua the space he desperately craved. Their home, a modest suburban house filled with the comforting smells of home-cooked meals, was a stark contrast to the dark, musty confines of the attic. Yet, for Joshua, it felt like another form of captivity, a constant surveillance of his every move and action.

The first few weeks were a blur of medical appointments, therapy sessions, and attempts at reintegrating him into a normal life. The doctors meticulously documented his physical condition – his emaciated frame, his weakened muscles, his stunted growth. The therapists, however, faced a far more daunting task: untangling the knots of trauma that had been woven into the fabric of his being. He struggled to communicate, his vocabulary limited, his ability to express emotions nearly nonexistent. His silences were deafening, punctuated only by the occasional tremor of his hands or the involuntary twitch of his eye.

His experiences within the foster
care system were, at first, a mixture
of overwhelming kindness and
simmering insecurity. There were
moments of genuine affection. Mrs.
Miller's gentle touch, as she brushed
his hair, brought a fleeting moment
of comfort; the warmth of Mr.
Miller's hand on his shoulder as he
sat beside him offered a sense of
protection and safety. He found a
strange comfort in the routine, the
predictability of their daily life, a
stark contrast to the erratic patterns
of his past. He was given nutritious
meals, clean clothes, and a warm
bed – simple comforts that he had
never experienced before. His
interactions with the Millers' teenage
children were tentative at first. Their
attempts at friendly conversation, at
including him in their family life,
felt awkward, clumsy, but well-
intentioned.

But beneath the surface, a profound sense of unease lingered. He found himself constantly on edge, hyper-vigilant, expecting the next blow, the next act of cruelty. He flinched at raised voices, recoiled from sudden movements, and retreated into himself at the slightest sign of displeasure. The slightest change in routine threw him into a state of anxiety, while his sleep was plagued by vivid nightmares that transported him back to the dark, cramped space where he had spent so many years of his life. His fear wasn't just a consequence of his past but a manifestation of his current circumstances: the fear of abandonment, the fear of being rejected, the fear of finding himself once again trapped and isolated.

His therapeutic sessions were a crucible of his emotions and memories. Initially, he was reluctant

to share anything. He would sit
silently, staring blankly ahead, his
gaze distant and vacant. Slowly,
painstakingly, his therapist guided
him through the process of
emotional recovery. They used play
therapy, art therapy, and narrative
therapy, techniques designed to help
him express himself in a way that
didn't require him to directly
confront his trauma. The process
was slow, agonizing, and marked by
periods of regression and setbacks.
He would cling to the few moments
of stability he had found with the
Millers, and then recoil at the
prospect of moving on or forging
new relationships.

The social workers assigned to his
case were a source of both support
and frustration. Their visits were a
constant reminder of the system that
had failed him, a reminder that he
was still an object of bureaucratic

scrutiny rather than a child in need of care. They documented every aspect of his progress (or lack thereof), filled countless forms, and attended numerous meetings. Their attempts to understand his situation were well-intentioned but often fell short, their language of social work terms falling far short of understanding his reality.

After six months, the Millers' adopted him. They continued to face unexpected challenges. The scars, both physical and emotional, were deeply entrenched. Joshua struggled at school, displaying symptoms of PTSD – nightmares, flashbacks, and emotional outbursts. He had difficulty forming relationships with his peers, often retreating into isolation, haunted by the specter of his past. Despite the challenges, however, the Millers remained unwavering in their support. They became his anchors in a world that still felt chaotic and unstable, their love a beacon guiding him through the darkness. But it was a long journey, a process filled with setbacks and breakthroughs. He learned to trust, bit by bit, to open his heart, inch by inch. He began to understand that not all adults were threats. He learned the meaning of a home and the solace of true family. The fire, the ordeal, the years of confinement – these had become, despite their horrors, the catalyst for his emergence. He was alive. He was loved. He would, one day, be truly free.

Chapter 3: Healing Begins

The first time Joshua saw his reflection, it was less a shock and more a confirmation of the whispers he'd heard – a ghost in the mirror staring back. His skin, stretched taut over bone, clung to his frame like a discarded shroud. His ribs were a roadmap etched across his chest, each indentation a stark reminder of the starvation he had endured. His eyes, once bright and full of life, were now sunken, shadowed hollows that reflected the emptiness within. His limbs were thin, his muscles atrophied, reduced to wisps beneath his paper-thin skin. He weighed ninety pounds, a statistic that spoke volumes of the horrific neglect he had suffered.

The initial medical examinations were a blur of prodding and poking, a cold invasion that triggered waves of anxiety. Doctors spoke in hushed tones, their voices filled with a mix of professional detachment and quiet horror. They noted his severe malnutrition, his stunted growth, the myriad of physical problems caused by years of deprivation. He was diagnosed with rickets, a condition caused by vitamin D deficiency, which had left his bones weakened and deformed. His teeth were decayed and rotting, the result of a diet devoid of proper nutrients. His immune system was severely compromised, leaving him vulnerable to infection. His digestive system, too, was badly damaged, rendering it unable to process normal food.

His recovery began slowly, painstakingly. The first few weeks were a struggle. He was fed intravenously, his body unable to cope with solid food. The nurses, ever so gentle, would monitor his vital signs, adjusting the drips, soothing his anxieties. The smallest amount of food would trigger nausea and vomiting, a testament to the brutal damage inflicted upon his digestive system. He remembered the metallic taste of the intravenous fluids, an unwelcome but necessary intrusion. He was initially hesitant to even attempt to eat, a lingering fear of rejection, of being punished, preventing him from accepting the nourishment offered.

The physical therapy sessions were equally grueling. His muscles, weakened from years of inactivity, were atrophied and atrophied. The simplest of movements – raising an arm, flexing a leg – were met with pain, with his body protesting in spasms of agony. The therapist, a kind woman with boundless patience, worked with him gently, slowly building up his strength, starting with tiny movements, tiny stretches. Each session was a battle against his own body, a fight to regain control, to reclaim the basic functions that had been denied to him. The therapist's touch, initially dreaded, became a source of small comfort, a gentle reminder of the human contact he so desperately craved. His body was slowly regaining its strength, his muscles starting to recover, his ability to move improving gradually. The pain was a constant companion, but so was the sense of progress.

The emotional toll was as significant as the physical. The pain, the discomfort, the procedures – all were a constant reminder of his captivity. His nightmares persisted, vivid and terrifying, forcing him to relive the darkness of the attic, the chill of the floor, the haunting silence punctuated by the sounds of his tormentors. He'd jolt awake, his heart racing, his body drenched in sweat, the memory of his confinement clinging to him like a second skin. During the day, he found it challenging to remain calm, exhibiting signs of extreme anxiety – a rapid heartbeat, trembling hands, and moments of acute distress. The slightest noise, the sudden appearance of a shadow, would trigger immediate panic.

He would often withdraw, retreating into himself, finding solace only in the quiet solitude of his hospital room. The nurses would find him curled up in a fetal position, his eyes closed tight, trying to find escape from his internal demons. They would approach him quietly, speaking softly, gently attempting to provide him some comfort and reassurance. He would remain silent, unable to articulate his feelings, his trauma too deep-seated to be expressed.

His diet was carefully planned by a nutritionist who worked in tandem with his doctors. The process was slow, methodical, tailored to address his severe malnutrition and compromised digestive system. He started with clear liquids, gradually transitioning to softer foods, eventually making his way to regular meals. The nutritionist would explain the importance of a balanced diet, the necessity of adequate protein, vitamins, and minerals, and he would watch, with his characteristic stoicism, the gradual changes in his physical condition. Each meal was a step towards recovery, a fight against the physical and psychological scars of his past.

The support system surrounding Joshua was extensive. The social workers, the doctors, the nurses, the physical therapists – all worked tirelessly to rebuild his life, to provide him with the care he so desperately needed. The Millers, his adoptive parents, visited regularly, bringing him small comforts – books, toys, and soft blankets – symbols of the new life that lay ahead. They talked to him softly, they read to him quietly, they reassured him of their constant presence, the presence of love and support. Their dedication, their patience, and their unwavering commitment helped turn his recovery into a journey of healing rather than an endless uphill battle.

The progress was slow but steady. The visible improvements were a reflection of the unseen battles he fought daily. The increased strength in his muscles, the improved condition of his teeth, the improved digestion, all were signs of his remarkable resilience, his strength, his determination to survive. He was recovering physically, but there was still a long road ahead, both physically and emotionally. His path to recovery was a long journey, a testament to his enduring spirit, and the unwavering support of those who cared. His physical recovery was only the first step towards reclaiming his life, toward embracing a future he had previously believed was impossible. The physical scars would remain, a reminder of his past, but they would not define his future. He was learning to walk, to run, to live again. And the strength and resilience he showed in the process would stand as an example for all.

The first session with Dr. Aris was a blur. Joshua sat rigidly on the edge of the plush armchair, his small frame swallowed by the oversized cushions. He clutched his hands together, his knuckles white, his eyes darting nervously around the room. Dr. Aris, a woman with kind eyes and a gentle smile, spoke softly, her voice a calming balm in the otherwise sterile environment. She didn't push; she simply observed, allowing Joshua to acclimate to her presence, to the strange feeling of being seen, truly seen, for the first time in years. He hadn't spoken a word, offering only terse nods or the occasional shake of his head in response to her questions. The silence stretched, thick and heavy, punctuated only by the ticking of the clock, a relentless rhythm that mirrored the beat of his anxious heart. He found the silence almost worse than the questions, a suffocating void that amplified his internal turmoil. The comfortable silence was eventually broken by a small cough from Joshua, a thin, reedy sound barely audible above the ticking clock. Dr. Aris immediately picked up on it, her eyes softening with concern.

The initial sessions focused on building trust, on creating a safe space where Joshua felt comfortable enough to begin sharing his experiences. Dr. Aris used play therapy, employing dolls and building blocks to help him express his emotions non-verbally. He would often build elaborate towers, only to knock them down in a fit of rage, his silent fury a stark representation of the inner turmoil he was struggling to contain. She would sit quietly, observing his actions, offering gentle encouragement without forcing him to articulate his feelings. The blocks became a metaphor for his shattered life, each carefully constructed tower representing a fragile hope, easily destroyed by the weight of his trauma.

One day, he started drawing. His initial sketches were hesitant, shaky lines, devoid of color, reflecting the bleakness of his memories. Slowly, though, the drawings began to change. Colors crept into his work, hesitant at first, then bolder, more vibrant. He drew pictures of the attic, depicting its darkness, its cramped confines, the chill of the floorboards. He drew pictures of his mother, her face obscured, her features indeterminate, a haunting reflection of his ambivalent feelings toward her. He drew pictures of himself, initially as a stick figure, frail and vulnerable, gradually evolving into a more defined self-portrait, a testament to his growing sense of self. The drawings were not merely therapeutic tools; they were a visual diary, chronicling his journey from despair to hope.

As the weeks passed, Joshua began to open up, albeit gradually. He would tell Dr. Aris about the hunger, the cold, the isolation. He would describe the constant fear, the feeling of being trapped, of being invisible. He would talk about the nightmares, the vivid images that haunted his sleep, the sounds that echoed in his memory. His words were hesitant, his voice often trembling, but the stories began to flow, each session unveiling a deeper layer of his trauma. Dr. Aris listened patiently, without judgment, her presence a constant source of support and reassurance. She validated his feelings, assuring him that his experiences were not his fault, that he was not alone in his suffering. She taught him coping mechanisms for managing his anxiety and flashbacks. She helped him to recognize and understand his triggers, teaching him techniques to manage his emotional responses when faced with difficult situations.

His foster home with the Millers was a haven of stability and support. Mr. and Mrs. Miller were kind, patient, and understanding. They never pushed him to talk about his past; instead, they created a nurturing environment where he felt safe and loved. They encouraged his interests, providing him with books, games, and opportunities to explore his creativity. They allowed him to set his own pace, recognizing the importance of gradual healing. They celebrated his small victories, his progress, no matter how incremental. Their consistent support was integral to his emotional healing. They were present without prying, always there with encouragement and unwavering love. They offered him routine and stability, something he had been denied for so long. The consistent presence of a loving family was something that had been totally absent from his life before, so the routine was a quiet but powerful healing experience in itself.

Therapy was not a linear process. There were setbacks, periods of regression, moments of overwhelming despair. There were days when he would withdraw completely, unable to face the pain of his memories. There were days when he would lash out in anger, his frustration and rage spilling over in unpredictable ways. Dr. Aris worked through these challenges with him, providing him with tools and strategies to manage his emotions. She taught him mindfulness techniques, helping him to focus on the present moment, to ground himself in reality, rather than being consumed by the past. She helped him develop healthy coping mechanisms to deal with his trauma, encouraging him to participate in activities that brought him joy and a sense of accomplishment. She also encouraged him to engage in physical activities to help him manage his trauma-related symptoms.

One particular breakthrough occurred during a session when Joshua was drawing a picture of a bird. He explained that the bird represented freedom. As he talked about the bird, his voice cracked with emotion, and he began to cry. It was the first time he had openly expressed such intense emotion since his rescue. Dr. Aris held his hand, her touch offering comfort and support. He spoke of his longing for freedom, for a life free from fear and oppression. He acknowledged the darkness he had endured, but also his determination to overcome it. The bird drawing marked a turning point. It was a visual expression of his resilience, his determination to take flight and soar into a brighter future.

As Joshua's trust in Dr. Aris grew, so too did his capacity to confront his trauma. He started to engage in more challenging therapeutic exercises, working through his feelings of anger, betrayal, and abandonment. He learned to identify his triggers, and to develop strategies for managing his anxiety. He began to confront the complex emotions he held toward his mother,

grappling with feelings of both
anger and sadness. The process was
neither quick nor easy; it was a long,
arduous journey filled with
emotional ups and downs. It wasn't
just about processing the past, but
actively rebuilding himself and his
life.

The journey was a marathon, not a
sprint. There were days of progress,
and days of setbacks. But each step,
no matter how small, moved him
closer to healing. He learned to trust
again, not only in others, but also in
himself. He learned that healing
wasn't a destination, but a
continuous process. It was a journey
of self-discovery, of self-acceptance,
and of self-forgiveness. He was
reclaiming his life, piece by piece,
day by day. The road ahead
remained long, but the path was
clearer, and he felt capable, stronger,
and filled with the quiet

determination to continue walking forward. The scars remained, but they no longer defined him. They were a testament to his resilience, a reminder of the strength he possessed. He was healing, and that was enough for now.

The Millers' house wasn't grand, but it felt like a castle to Joshua. It smelled of freshly baked bread and sunshine, a stark contrast to the stale, musty odor of the attic. He found himself drawn to the scent, to the warmth of the kitchen, where Mrs. Miller often hummed as she prepared meals. He initially watched from a distance, a shy observer, his movements hesitant and his eyes downcast. He ate his meals quickly, barely making eye contact, as if afraid that any interaction would shatter the fragile peace he had found. He seemed to anticipate rejection, a reflex

ingrained in him from years of
isolation.

Mr. Miller, a man with kind eyes
and a reassuring smile, started by
introducing Joshua to simple tasks.
He'd ask him to help with setting
the table or watering the plants.
These small gestures were
significant; they were a form of
inclusion, an invitation to participate
in the family's daily routine. It was a
subtle demonstration of trust, a
silent assurance that he was a valued
member of their household. Joshua,
initially resistant, slowly began to
respond. He would nod, a shy
acceptance, his movements still
tentative, but his participation
palpable.

Weekends were different. On
Saturdays, Mr. Miller would take
Joshua to the park, a place that
initially filled him with
apprehension. The sounds, the

smells, the sheer number of people, all contributed to his anxiety. But Mr. Miller was patient, allowing Joshua to set the pace. They started with short walks, simple games of catch, gradually building Joshua's confidence and comfort levels. He'd allow Joshua to sit on the park bench, observing the world around him, offering a gentle word or a warm smile of encouragement without demanding interaction. Over time, Joshua began to engage more, participating in the activities, although his interactions remained limited. He'd sometimes throw the ball, his throws initially hesitant but eventually stronger and more confident. He'd cautiously interact with other children, though he preferred the company of Mr. Miller.

Sundays were for family dinners. These were daunting at first. The boisterous conversation, the laughter, the close proximity, all threatened to overwhelm him. He would sit quietly, eating quickly and barely making eye contact, retreating into himself. Mrs. Miller noticed and subtly adjusted. She wouldn't try to force him to engage, instead including him in small ways; she might ask him about his day, or his favorite book, offering a gentle opening for communication. The casual questions weren't meant to extract information, but to demonstrate that he was noticed, that he was important, that he was part of the family.

One Sunday, Mr. Miller brought home a board game. Joshua had never played one before. He initially resisted, retreating to his corner, but the warmth of the family's engagement was contagious. Slowly, tentatively, he joined in. He was clumsy at first, making mistakes, but

Mr. Miller patiently explained the rules, his voice calm and reassuring. As the game progressed, Joshua's hesitancy lessened; the game became a bridge, a shared experience that slowly eroded the barriers between him and his foster family. The laughter that erupted when he made a silly move was both disarming and comforting. It was a sound he hadn't heard in years, and it offered a profound sense of belonging.

Building trust with his social worker, Ms. Evans, proved to be a different challenge. Ms. Evans was a professional, efficient, and her approach was direct, yet compassionate. She understood Joshua's need for space and respect his boundaries. Their initial meetings were structured, focused on practical concerns—appointments, school, therapy— keeping the conversations short and

concise. Ms. Evans recognized that
Joshua needed time to build trust
and was never pushy.

Over time, Ms. Evans found ways to
connect with Joshua. She would
bring him small gifts—a book, a
drawing pad—simple tokens that
conveyed her care. She would ask
about his interests, his hobbies. She
never delved into his past unless he
initiated the conversation. The
subtle approach, respectful of his
vulnerabilities, fostered a sense of
security. The occasional visit
wouldn't feel intrusive or like an
interrogation. The careful balance
she held between professionalism
and compassion was remarkable.
She recognized that healing couldn't
be rushed; it was a process that
required patience, understanding,
and, above all, trust. She also
ensured that the interactions never

felt like formal interviews; they were relaxed and comforting.

One day, she brought him a small, battered wooden bird, a hand-carved trinket. Joshua was surprised; it was a simple gift, yet it resonated deeply. The bird reminded him of the drawing he had made in therapy, a symbol of his yearning for freedom. He didn't say anything, but he clutched the bird tightly in his hand, a silent acknowledgment of Ms. Evans's understanding and empathy. It was a small gesture, yet it represented a significant step in their evolving relationship, a silent understanding that transcended the professional boundaries.

School was another arena where Joshua had to navigate new relationships. The other children were curious, some friendly, some wary. He initially kept to himself, sitting alone at lunch, avoiding eye contact. The other children were initially unsure how to react to his quiet demeanor and withdrawn personality. They saw a boy who clearly carried invisible wounds; their curiosity mixed with caution. There was a sense of not wanting to pry or cause him any discomfort. He was slowly learning the social cues and dynamics that come naturally to most children, as years of isolation had left him struggling to understand the basic mechanics of socializing.

His teacher, Ms. Rodriguez, was patient and understanding. She approached him slowly, allowing him to acclimate to the school environment. She made sure his classes were not overly stimulating or demanding, recognizing the effect that sudden changes had on him. She would often sit with him during recess, talking softly about his interests. The slow, steady integration made all the difference. He responded to her kindness and understanding, beginning to engage in class and participate in group activities, albeit cautiously. He wasn't ready for friendships, but he was gradually building trust and tolerance for interactions.

The relationships Joshua built were not easy; they were a testament to his resilience, his determination to heal, and the unwavering support he received from his foster family and support system. These relationships were not forged overnight; they were carefully constructed, brick by brick, moment by moment. It was a painstaking process, fraught with challenges, setbacks, and moments of doubt. But the steady progress, however small, was a beacon of hope, illuminating his path towards a brighter future. He was learning that healing wasn't about erasing the past, but about integrating it into his present, transforming it into a source of strength, resilience, and ultimately, hope for the future. The slow, deliberate building of trust was the key, and it was finally taking root. He was finally beginning to feel safe, cared for, and loved. The journey was far from over, but he was finally walking it, not alone.

The school was a sensory overload at first. The cacophony of sounds, the bustling hallways, the sheer number of faces – it was overwhelming. Joshua found himself retreating into himself, his eyes darting around, his body tense. Lunchtime was particularly difficult. The crowded cafeteria, the chatter, the smells of various foods – it all felt suffocating. He'd sit alone, hunched over his tray, picking at his food, his gaze fixed on the floor. His initial attempts at communication were halting, his sentences short and hesitant, punctuated by long silences. The other children, initially curious, seemed hesitant to approach, sensing his vulnerability. They'd glance at him, some with pity, others with apprehension, but they stayed away, giving him the space he needed to acclimate.

Ms. Rodriguez, his teacher, was a beacon of calm amidst the chaos. She was patient, understanding, and never rushed him. She understood that his past had left him apprehensive, that the simple act of interacting could feel overwhelming. She didn't force interaction, instead, she gently nudged him towards participation. She'd start by simply acknowledging him, asking about his day in a soft, non-intrusive tone.

She'd ask him about his interests, listening attentively, validating his experiences, and ensuring him that he was safe and accepted. He found himself responding to her kindness, the gentle encouragement creating a sense of security. She started with small tasks, simple assignments that wouldn't overstimulate him. It was slow, painstaking progress, but it was progress, nonetheless.

Reading became a refuge for Joshua. Lost in the pages of a book, he could escape the overwhelming reality of his present. The stories offered solace, a distraction from the anxieties and insecurities that plagued him. He'd spend hours in the school library, surrounded by books, their silent stories offering a companionship he hadn't known before. Ms. Rodriguez recognized this and encouraged his love of reading. She started recommending books tailored to his interests, carefully selecting titles that would engage his imagination without overwhelming him. She also worked with the school librarian to ensure Joshua had access to the books he needed, setting up a special borrowing system to accommodate his specific needs.

Mathematics, surprisingly, proved to be a solace. The structured nature of math, the clear-cut rules, provided a sense of order and predictability in a world that often felt chaotic. He found a certain satisfaction in solving equations, in the logic and precision of mathematical operations. Ms. Rodriguez noticed this and incorporated mathematical games and puzzles into his lessons, transforming learning into a fun, engaging activity. He enjoyed the sense of accomplishment he felt when he solved a challenging problem, this quiet success boosting his self-confidence. This success translated to other areas, he started to participate more in class discussions, his contributions insightful and often unexpected.

Art class became another outlet for Joshua's pent-up emotions. He discovered a talent for sketching, his charcoal drawings depicting a range of emotions - sadness, hope, fear, and resilience. The act of creating, of transforming blank paper into something tangible, was cathartic. He'd often spend hours sketching, his movements slow and deliberate, his expressions focused and serene. His art teacher, Mr. Evans, recognized the depth of his talent and the therapeutic value of his art. He provided Joshua with individual guidance, encouraging his self-expression, creating a safe space for him to explore his emotions. He understood that Joshua wasn't just learning technique, but also processing his trauma, and his role was not just an instructor but also a facilitator of healing.

Slowly, tentatively, Joshua began to build connections with other children. It started with simple interactions – a shared smile, a brief conversation about a shared interest, a collaborative project. He was cautious, his interactions hesitant and brief, but they were interactions, nonetheless. He found himself drawn to children who were as quiet and introspective as he was. They connected on a deeper level, their shared experiences creating an unspoken bond. He learned to navigate the complex dynamics of friendships, his progress gradual but meaningful. It was a testament to his growing confidence and his burgeoning social skills.

After school, Joshua participated in a range of activities designed to enhance his independence and build his self-esteem. He started attending a local after-school program where he discovered a newfound passion for woodworking. The rhythmic nature of the work, the physicality of the task, and the tangible results provided a sense of accomplishment and control. He learned to build small wooden toys, each creation a small victory in his journey to self-reliance. The instructors at the program were skilled artisans who also acted as mentors. They encouraged his creativity, taught him valuable skills, and fostered his confidence. His newfound craft became a way to express himself, and the pride he felt in his creations was palpable. He even started selling his small creations at local craft fairs, a small business venture that taught him the value of hard work and the rewards of entrepreneurship.

Weekends were dedicated to exploring his community. The Millers encouraged his independence, allowing him to participate in activities that suited his interests. They would take him to the library, to the local museum, and to the park. He learned to use public transportation, gaining confidence in his ability to navigate his surroundings independently. They also enrolled him in several extracurricular activities. He joined a scouting group and learned survival skills that further reinforced his feeling of independence and self-reliance. The scouting trips out into the woods, spending time away from the house, gave him a new perspective, fostering his independence. His journey of recovery had multiple layers, physical, emotional, and psychological. He took these challenges one step at a time. He learned to trust again, to rely on himself, and to appreciate the simple pleasures of life.

His therapist, Dr. Albright, was instrumental in helping Joshua process his traumatic experiences. The therapy sessions were a safe space, a place where Joshua could confront his past without judgment. Dr. Albright used various therapeutic techniques to help Joshua cope with his PTSD, anxiety, and depression. He helped Joshua understand the impact of his trauma, teaching him coping mechanisms to manage his triggers and navigate his emotions. The healing wasn't easy, it was a long and often painful process, but Joshua persisted, driven by his determination to rebuild his life. He learned to identify and express his emotions, to recognize his own strengths and resilience.

Joshua's journey from the confines of the attic to the independence of his own life was slow, deliberate, and filled with challenges. But his progress was undeniable, a testament to his remarkable resilience and the unwavering support of those around him. The scars remained, but they were fading, slowly being replaced by a sense of hope, self-worth, and the promise of a future free from the shadows of his past. He was learning to live, to love, and to thrive. His journey wasn't over, but he was finally writing his own story, a story of resilience, hope, and ultimately, triumph.

The first time the memory surfaced, it was like a shard of glass piercing the carefully constructed calm of his life. He was in art class, sketching a bird, its wings outstretched in flight, a symbol of freedom he desperately craved. Suddenly, the image of the attic flooded his mind – the cramped space, the suffocating darkness, the chilling silence broken only by the occasional creak of the floorboards. The smell of mildew and dust, the gnawing hunger, the constant fear – it all came rushing back, overwhelming him with a wave of nausea and terror. His charcoal slipped from his trembling fingers, smudging the delicate lines of the bird's wing.

He excused himself from class, stumbling to the nearest restroom, his breaths shallow and ragged. He leaned against the cold tile wall, his body wracked with sobs. The memory, vivid and brutal, felt like a physical blow, tearing open wounds he thought he had carefully sutured. He was back in the attic, a small, helpless child, trapped and alone, his pleas for help swallowed by the silence. He felt the familiar knot of panic tightening in his chest, the suffocating weight of helplessness crushing his spirit.

Mr. Evans, his art teacher, found him huddled on the floor, his shoulders shaking. He didn't pry, didn't demand explanations. He simply knelt beside him, placing a comforting hand on his back. He offered him a tissue, a glass of water, and a quiet, understanding presence. He didn't speak, didn't rush him, simply allowed him to process the overwhelming emotions that threatened to consume him. This quiet acceptance, this unwavering support, was invaluable. It was a stark contrast to the silence and neglect he had endured in the attic, and it gave him the strength to breathe, to begin to cope.

The next few weeks were challenging. The memories, once dormant, now surfaced with increasing frequency. He found himself reliving moments of abuse, moments of terror, moments of profound loneliness. They came unbidden, uninvited, striking him at the most unexpected times – during a crowded school assembly, during a quiet moment of reading, during a seemingly ordinary conversation. Each time, the wave of panic was almost unbearable. He learned to recognize the warning signs – the tightening in his chest, the rapid heartbeat, the feeling of impending doom – and to employ the coping mechanisms Dr. Albright had taught

him. He'd retreat to a quiet place,
practice deep breathing exercises,
and focus on grounding techniques.
He'd visualize calming images,
listen to soothing music, and remind
himself that he was safe, that he was
loved, that he was no longer alone.

Dr. Albright's therapy sessions
became increasingly crucial. He
began to explore the details of his
trauma, articulating the memories
that had haunted him for so long.
He described the constant hunger,
the lack of hygiene, the emotional
and physical neglect. He talked
about the fear, the isolation, the
feeling of worthlessness. The process
was agonizingly slow, but with each
session, he felt a small sense of
release, a gradual lifting of the
weight that had burdened him for
years. He learned to identify his
triggers, the sights, sounds, and
smells that brought back the

memories, and to develop strategies for managing them.

He discovered the power of journaling. He began writing down his memories, his emotions, his fears. It was a way to externalize his pain, to give form and voice to the experiences that had long remained trapped inside. The act of writing became cathartic, a way to process his trauma, to make sense of the chaos. The words flowed, sometimes in a torrent, sometimes in a trickle, but they flowed, nonetheless. The pages of his journal became a repository of his pain, a testament to his resilience. He realized that by giving voice to his past, he was reclaiming his power, taking back control of his narrative.

He also found solace in art. He began to create pieces that reflected his experiences, his emotions. His art became a form of therapy, a way to express the things he couldn't articulate in words. His charcoal drawings became more intense, more visceral, depicting the darkness of his past, but also the glimmer of hope that was emerging. His paintings were a landscape of his inner world, a testament to his journey from despair to resilience. He began to use bright colors, bold strokes, and expressive forms, reflecting his growing confidence and his renewed sense of self.

The memories remained, but they no longer held the same power. They were still a part of his story, but they were no longer the whole story. He was learning to integrate them, to see them not as defining moments, but as moments that shaped him, strengthened him, made him who he was. He was learning to forgive, not just those who had hurt him, but also himself. He was learning to accept his past, to embrace his imperfections, and to move forward with hope and determination. He understood that healing wasn't a destination, but a journey, a continuous process of growth and self-discovery. The journey was far from over, but he was finally starting to feel the lightness of freedom, the warmth of self-acceptance, and the hope for a future filled with joy and possibility.

He began to dream again, vivid, colorful dreams that had nothing to do with the attic. He dreamt of soaring above the clouds, of running through fields of wildflowers, of laughing with friends. These dreams reflected his growing resilience, his ability to detach from the pain of the past and embrace the promise of the future. He began to see his life not as a series of traumatic events, but as a tapestry woven with threads of both darkness and light, sorrow and joy, pain and healing.

His relationships with the Millers deepened. He felt comfortable sharing more of his past with them, and they responded with unwavering love and support. They were a constant source of strength, a safe haven in the storm. They understood that healing took time, that there would be setbacks, but they never wavered in their commitment to him. They celebrated his small victories, offered comfort during his struggles, and provided an unconditional love that he desperately needed. Their patience, empathy, and understanding became crucial tools in his healing process. The Millers' home was no longer just a place of shelter; it had become a symbol of warmth, acceptance, and unconditional love—a stark contrast to the chilling emptiness of the attic.

He gradually started to rebuild trust, not just in others but, most importantly, in himself. The trust he'd lost, shattered by years of abuse and neglect, was slowly being restored, piece by piece, brick by brick. He was learning to recognize the signs of manipulation, to assert his boundaries, to say no when he needed to. He was learning to value himself, to believe in his own worth, to recognize his own strength. This newfound self-worth was the most powerful weapon in his arsenal against the lingering shadows of his past. He started setting goals, small attainable goals at first—like finishing a book, mastering a new skill, or making a new friend. Each accomplishment was a small but significant victory in his ongoing battle for healing and self-discovery.

The path to healing was not a straight line; it was a winding, often treacherous road, filled with unexpected twists and turns, moments of progress and setbacks, periods of intense emotion and quiet reflection. But with each step forward, however small, Joshua felt a renewed sense of purpose, a strengthened resolve, and an unshakeable belief in his ability to overcome the trauma he had endured. He was not merely surviving; he was thriving, building a life of his own, a life filled with hope, joy, and the unwavering promise of a future free from the shadows of the past. His story was one of resilience, not just in overcoming adversity, but in rebuilding a life from the ashes of his past, a life where he was the author of his own destiny. His journey of healing was a testament to the indomitable spirit of a child

who had faced unimaginable
horrors and emerged, not broken,
but stronger, more resilient, and
ultimately, triumphant.

Chapter 4: A New Beginning

The crisp autumn air nipped at Joshua's cheeks as he walked across the sprawling campus of the community college. He'd chosen a surprisingly practical path—automotive technology—a field that demanded precision and focus, qualities he was diligently cultivating. The rhythmic clang of metal on metal in the workshop was a soothing counterpoint to the persistent whispers of his past. The hands that once trembled with fear now moved with surprising dexterity, guided by a newfound sense of purpose. He found a strange solace in the mechanics of engines, the tangible results of his efforts a welcome contrast to the intangible wounds of his past.

His grades were excellent, a testament to his unwavering

dedication. He studied late into the night, fueled by coffee and a fierce determination to prove to himself, and to the world, that he was more than the sum of his trauma. He wasn't just surviving; he was thriving, proving his resilience with every wrench he turned, every engine he repaired. Each successful project was a small victory, a concrete symbol of his progress, a tangible reminder that he was building a future, a future he was actively crafting with his own hands.

The support system that had helped him through the darkest days remained vital. The Millers were his steadfast anchors, their unwavering love and support a constant presence in his life. They attended his open house, beaming with pride as they watched him effortlessly engage with his instructors and peers. Their presence was a silent affirmation of his worth, a constant reminder that he was loved, accepted, and cherished. They celebrated his academic achievements as if they were their own, their unwavering belief in him fueling his own confidence. He still needed them, even now, but the need felt less desperate, more like a comforting reliance on a trusted foundation.

His relationship with Dr. Albright continued, though the sessions were less frequent and less focused on the trauma itself. They now delved into issues of self-esteem, trust, and healthy relationship dynamics. He was learning to navigate the complexities of social interactions, to decipher subtle cues, to identify manipulative behavior, and to set healthy boundaries. Dr. Albright helped him unpack the lingering effects of isolation, teaching him the importance of communication, assertiveness, and the power of vulnerability in forming authentic connections. It was a gradual process, filled with moments of hesitation and uncertainty, but each session strengthened his ability to navigate the world with greater confidence and self-awareness.

While his academic pursuits flourished, the emotional scars of his past still surfaced unexpectedly. Sometimes, the scent of mildew would trigger a wave of nausea and panic, transporting him back to the suffocating darkness of the attic. Other times, the sound of raised voices would evoke a primal fear, a visceral reminder of the violence that had permeated his childhood. He learned to anticipate these triggers and to employ coping mechanisms—deep breathing

exercises, grounding techniques,
and the comforting routine of his art.
He continued to write a journal,
chronicling his progress, his
setbacks, and the ongoing process of
healing. His writing was no longer
simply a cathartic release; it was a
powerful tool for self-reflection and
growth. It was a way to track his
journey, to see the progress he had
made, and to appreciate the strength
he had cultivated.

His artistic expression evolved,
reflecting the complexities of his
emotional journey. He experimented
with different mediums, finding
solace in the fluidity of watercolors,
the precision of pen and ink, the
power of sculpting clay. His art
became a testament to his resilience,
capturing not only the darkness of
his past but also the beauty and
hope that was now blooming in his
life. He began to showcase his work,

first in small local exhibitions, then in college art shows. The positive feedback he received bolstered his self-esteem, validating his artistic talent and reminding him of his capacity for creativity and self-expression.

He also started exploring relationships, but cautiously, deliberately. He'd formed friendships with classmates, sharing his interests, his struggles, and his hopes for the future. These relationships were built on mutual respect, understanding, and trust—qualities he actively cultivated and cherished. He was learning the delicate art of intimacy, realizing that vulnerability was not weakness but a source of strength. His connections with these friends, however, differed significantly from the toxic family relationships he had experienced. These friendships offered support, shared laughter, and a sense of belonging, a stark contrast to the isolating environment of his captivity. He recognized and appreciated the value of genuine connection, and the friendships he built provided a powerful counter-narrative to the years of isolation and emotional neglect.

One evening, while working on a particularly challenging engine repair, he experienced a flashback so intense it brought him to his knees. The smell of gasoline, oddly similar to the mildew of his past, triggered a torrent of memories—the cramped space, the gnawing hunger, the chilling fear. The workshop seemed to shrink around him, the metallic clang fading into the oppressive silence of the attic. He felt the familiar tightening in his chest, the overwhelming sense of helplessness. He recognized the warning signs immediately and moved to a quiet corner, focusing on his breathing exercises. He knew this was a setback, but he didn't let it define him. He allowed himself to process the emotions, acknowledging the pain, without judgment or self-criticism.

The next morning, he returned to the workshop, his determination undeterred. He faced the engine, not with fear, but with a quiet resolve. He completed the repair, his movements precise and assured, a testament to his ability to confront and overcome his trauma. The incident, while difficult, served as a reminder that healing wasn't a linear process—it was a journey filled with moments of progress and regression. The key he learned was to acknowledge the setbacks, to learn from them, and to move forward with renewed determination. His ability to approach his trauma with self-compassion and resilience spoke volumes of his progress and inner strength.

Joshua's journey was a testament to the human capacity for resilience, demonstrating that even the deepest wounds can heal, given the right support, time, and unwavering self-belief. He was not only reclaiming his life but actively building a future filled with purpose, hope, and a profound appreciation for the simple joys of human connection and fulfillment. The shadows of his past would always be a part of his story, but they no longer held the power to define him. He was now the author of his own narrative, his life a testament to the enduring strength of the human spirit. He was living proof that even from the darkest depths of despair, one could find the light, embrace hope, and ultimately, create a life worth living.

The decision to speak out hadn't been a sudden epiphany, a dramatic unveiling. It had been a slow, deliberate unfurling, like a delicate flower pushing through hardened earth. It began with small, tentative steps, whispered confidences shared with Dr. Albright, hesitant words etched into the pages of his journal. He started by narrating the mundane details of his days at the community college, the satisfying precision of repairing engines, the camaraderie he found among his classmates. These seemingly insignificant details, however, were building blocks, laying the foundation for something larger, something more profound. He realized that by sharing the ordinary, the everyday victories, he was subtly chipping away at the walls of silence that had imprisoned him for so long.

One day, Dr. Albright suggested he try writing a short story, a fictionalized account of his experience. Initially, the idea felt daunting, even absurd. How could he possibly translate the horrors of his past into something palatable, something that could be read, understood, and perhaps even empathized with? The very notion of putting his trauma into words felt like a betrayal, a violation. But as he began to write, something shifted within him. The act of transforming his pain into narrative gave him a sense of control, a feeling of empowerment he hadn't experienced before. The fictionalized elements allowed him a distance, a buffer, yet the raw emotion, the visceral fear and despair, still resonated on the page.

He discovered a surprising freedom
in the act of writing, a cathartic
release that transcended therapy
sessions. The words flowed,
sometimes in a torrent, other times
in a trickle, but they flowed,
nonetheless. He found himself
rewriting passages, refining
sentences, crafting the narrative with
meticulous care. The writing itself
became a form of therapy, a process
of self-discovery and healing. Each
completed page was a small step
towards reclaiming his narrative,
away from the shadows of his past
and towards the illumination of his
present.

His initial story, a short piece about
a boy who escapes from a dark
room, was met with encouraging
feedback from Dr. Albright. The
doctor praised his evocative prose,
his ability to convey raw emotion
with restraint, and his capacity to

weave the darkness with moments of unexpected hope. This validation was crucial, a silent affirmation that his voice, his story, was not only worth hearing but valuable. The positive response emboldened him to write more, to delve deeper into the details of his captivity, to explore the complex emotional landscape of his experiences.

The next story was longer, more intricate, more revealing. He still employed fictional elements, but the core of the narrative remained grounded in his reality. He wrote about the hunger, the constant cold, the crushing loneliness, but he also wrote about the small moments of hope, the glimpses of light that filtered through the cracks in his prison. He wrote about the resilience of the human spirit, the unwavering determination to survive, to endure, to find a sliver of joy amidst unimaginable pain.

As he continued to write, he realized that his motivation went beyond personal healing. He recognized a profound responsibility to share his story, to give voice to the voiceless, to shed light on the systemic failures that had allowed his abuse to occur. He understood that he could prevent such horrors from befalling other children by speaking out. His tale wasn't just his own; it was a reflection of the thousands of children trapped in similar situations, silently suffering in the shadows.

The decision to go public wasn't easy. Doubt gnawed at him, whispering insidious fears in his ear. What if people didn't believe him? What if he was ridiculed or judged? What if reliving the trauma overwhelmed him? These fears were valid, tangible threats, but they were counterbalanced by an even stronger force—the desire to make a difference, to effect change, to give a voice to the silent victims.

He began by sharing his story with close friends and family, testing the waters, gauging their reactions. The Millers listened patiently, their unwavering support bolstering his resolve. They offered practical assistance, helping him to navigate the complexities of publishing, and emotional support, helping him to manage the anxieties that accompanied his decision. Their confidence in him was unwavering, a beacon of hope that guided him through the turbulent waters of self-doubt.

He then reached out to a local journalist, a woman known for her insightful and compassionate reporting on social issues. He had found her articles on child abuse particularly poignant, her words resonant with empathy and understanding. He shared his manuscript with her, entrusting her with his deepest fears and darkest secrets. The journalist listened attentively, responding not with pity but with admiration and respect. She understood the power of his story, the vital importance of sharing his experiences with the world.

The subsequent article was a sensation, attracting national attention. Joshua's story ignited a firestorm of public outrage, prompting investigations into the failures of the child protection system, and demanding reforms to prevent similar tragedies. He became an advocate, a spokesperson for the voiceless, a symbol of resilience and hope. He traveled to schools, giving speeches to students, reminding them of the importance of reporting suspected abuse. He met with legislators, lobbying for stricter laws and increased funding for child protection services.

His life, once defined by isolation and despair, was now filled with purpose and meaning. The act of sharing his story had transformed him, stripping away the shame and self-blame that had clung to him like a shroud. He realized that his trauma didn't define him; it was a part of his story, but not the whole of it. He was more than a victim; he was a survivor, a warrior, a beacon of hope for others who had endured similar ordeals.

The response to his story was overwhelming, a torrent of emails, phone calls, and letters from people who had been touched by his words. He received messages from survivors, expressing gratitude for his bravery, his willingness to share his truth. He received messages from parents, pledging to be more vigilant and protective of their children. He received messages from lawmakers, committing to enact changes to protect vulnerable children.

He learned that speaking out had been not only a courageous act but a profoundly liberating one. The weight of his past, once crushing, had been lifted, replaced by a sense of lightness, a feeling of freedom he had never known. The act of sharing his narrative, of reclaiming his story, had given him back his voice, his power, his life. He had stared into the abyss of his past and had not only survived but had emerged stronger, wiser, and more determined than ever. His voice, once silenced, now echoed with strength and conviction, a powerful testament to the indomitable human spirit, a testament to the enduring power of hope, even in the darkest of circumstances. The scars remained, etched into his memory, but they no longer defined him. They were merely a reminder of the journey he had undertaken, the battles he had won, the life he had reclaimed. He was no longer just surviving; he was thriving. He was living.

The national attention brought a whirlwind of activity into Joshua's life. He wasn't just a survivor anymore; he was a symbol, a beacon of hope for countless others. His quiet life in the small college town was replaced by a schedule packed with interviews, speeches, and meetings. He found himself traveling across the country, sharing his story with anyone who would listen—school children, legislators, and even skeptical journalists who initially questioned the veracity of his claims. Each time he spoke, a part of him healed further. The act of sharing, of bearing witness to his own suffering, became a powerful catalyst for his own recovery.

One of his most impactful engagements was a speech he delivered at a national conference on child abuse prevention. He stood on the stage, a small figure against the vast backdrop, his voice surprisingly strong, and recounted his ordeal. He spoke not just of his personal experience but of the systemic failings that had allowed his abuse to continue for so long. He highlighted the lack of communication between agencies, the inadequate training of social workers, and the overwhelming caseloads that left many vulnerable children overlooked and neglected.

His words, raw and honest, resonated with the audience, a mixture of social workers, child advocates, and lawmakers. The silence following his speech was deafening, broken only by the occasional sniffle or a choked sob.

Following the conference, he was inundated with requests for interviews. He spoke to national news outlets, sharing his story with millions. He wasn't afraid to delve into the uncomfortable details, the horrific realities of his confinement, the constant hunger, the pervasive fear, the soul-crushing loneliness. He spoke of the moments he felt the closest to giving up, the times when hope seemed to flicker and die. But he also spoke of the small, almost imperceptible moments of resilience, the flicker of light that somehow managed to pierce through the darkness, the strength that he discovered within himself, the will to survive.

These interviews weren't just about recounting his ordeal; they were about advocating for change. He became a tireless advocate for stronger child protection laws, demanding improved training for social workers, increased funding for child protective services, and mandatory reporting laws that would hold adults accountable for neglecting or abusing children. He argued for a system that prioritized the well-being of children above all else, a system that listened to their voices, believed their stories, and acted swiftly and decisively to protect them.

His advocacy extended beyond the media spotlight. He became actively involved in lobbying efforts, meeting with lawmakers to push for legislation that would reform child welfare systems. He meticulously researched the existing laws, identifying loopholes and weaknesses that needed to be addressed. He presented lawmakers with detailed proposals, backed by data and research, demonstrating the urgent need for reform. He patiently answered their questions, patiently explained his experiences and the impact of such laws on children's lives. He became a voice for the voiceless, armed with compelling evidence and an unwavering commitment to justice.

His work wasn't limited to legislative action. He partnered with several non-profit organizations that worked with child abuse survivors. He shared his story at fundraising events, inspiring donors to support critical initiatives such as counseling services, trauma-informed care, and residential programs for children who had experienced abuse. He lent his name and his story to countless campaigns to bring awareness to the issue. He became a symbol of hope and resilience, proving that even after enduring unimaginable suffering, it was possible to heal, to thrive, and to make a difference.

The impact of his advocacy was significant and far-reaching. His story triggered investigations into the systems that had failed him, revealing widespread inadequacies and negligence. His outspokenness led to policy changes, improved training for social workers, and increased funding for child protection programs. His relentless pursuit of justice brought to light critical loopholes in the existing laws and highlighted the need for comprehensive reforms. He played a crucial role in shaping legislation that improved the lives of countless vulnerable children.

One of the most gratifying outcomes of Joshua's advocacy was the establishment of a national hotline dedicated specifically to helping children who were in dangerous situations. This hotline was a direct result of the public outcry triggered by his story. He was instrumental in ensuring that the hotline was staffed by trained professionals who could provide immediate support, guidance, and resources to children in need. The creation of this vital resource offered a lifeline to children who were too afraid or too isolated to speak up. It stood as a powerful testament to his commitment to making a difference, his belief in the power of collective action to protect children.

Joshua understood that his advocacy was not just a job but a personal mission. It was driven by his unwavering conviction that no child should ever experience the kind of trauma he had endured. His actions were fueled by a desire to leave the world a better place for those who were most vulnerable, a world where every child had a safe and loving home.

His advocacy also involved supporting other survivors. He actively sought out opportunities to connect with other individuals who had experienced similar traumas. He shared his experiences, offering support and guidance. He shared his strategies for coping with PTSD and other lingering effects of trauma. He helped them find the strength to speak out, to reclaim their lives and their voices. He understood that the journey to healing was not a solitary

one; it was a journey best taken
together.

His work wasn't without its
challenges. There were moments of
doubt, when the weight of his
responsibilities threatened to
overwhelm him. There were times
when the memories resurfaced, the
trauma threatened to consume him
once more. But he found strength in
his purpose, in his conviction that
his efforts were making a difference.
He found solace in the support of his
friends and family, the unwavering
belief of Dr. Albright, and the
countless messages of gratitude he
received from survivors and their
families.

Joshua's journey wasn't about
achieving vengeance or seeking
retribution. It was about prevention,
about creating a better future for
children. He used his experience to
fuel his activism, turning his pain

into a powerful force for change. He transformed his suffering into a vehicle for advocacy, demonstrating the resilience of the human spirit and the profound capacity for hope and healing, even in the darkest of circumstances. His story wasn't just about surviving; it was about thriving and ensuring that others had the opportunity to do the same. His legacy was not etched in the scars of his past but in the positive changes he brought to the world, making a profound and lasting impact on the lives of countless children. The boy who had once been trapped in an attic had emerged as a powerful voice for change, a testament to the indomitable spirit that can overcome even the most profound adversity. He was a living embodiment of hope, a shining example of how trauma can be transformed into a force for good, a symbol of resilience, a champion for the voiceless. His journey, far from being over, was an ongoing testament to the enduring power of the human spirit.

The relentless pace of advocacy eventually began to take its toll. The constant reminders of his past, the interviews, the speeches, the meetings—they were all necessary, even vital, but they chipped away at his fragile peace. He found himself wrestling with a new kind of exhaustion, one that went beyond physical fatigue. It was a weariness of the soul, a deep-seated tiredness that threatened to overwhelm him. He realized he needed to take a step back, to find a space where he could simply be Joshua, not the symbol, not the advocate, but simply the man who had survived.

He sought refuge in the quiet solitude of his small cabin nestled deep within the woods, miles away from the clamor of city life and the constant demands of his public persona. The cabin, a gift from a grateful benefactor, offered a sanctuary, a place where he could disconnect from the outside world and reconnect with himself. Here, surrounded by the whispering pines and the calming rhythm of nature, he began the arduous work of self-discovery and healing.

It wasn't a linear process. Some days were better than others. Some days, the memories would flood back with excruciating clarity, the cold, damp confines of the attic, the gnawing hunger, the crushing weight of loneliness. On these days, he would allow himself to grieve, to feel the full force of the pain, without judgment or self-reproach. He had learned that suppressing his emotions only prolonged the healing process. He learned to embrace his feelings, acknowledging them as part of his story, not as defining elements of his identity.

He found solace in the simple act of being present, of breathing in the crisp forest air, feeling the warmth of the sun on his skin, listening to the songs of birds. He discovered a newfound appreciation for the beauty of the natural world, a beauty that had been denied to him for so long. He spent hours hiking through the woods, finding peace in the solitude of the trails, allowing the rhythm of his footsteps to soothe his troubled mind.

His therapist, Dr. Albright, had been instrumental in guiding him through this crucial phase of his recovery. She emphasized the importance of self-compassion, of treating himself with the same kindness and understanding that he showed others. She encouraged him to practice mindfulness, to focus on the present moment rather than dwelling on the past or worrying about the future. She helped him understand that forgiveness, both of himself and of his abusers, was not about condoning their actions but about freeing himself from the shackles of resentment and anger.

Forgiveness wasn't a single event, but a gradual process, a series of small steps toward acceptance. It began with forgiving himself for the feelings of helplessness and self-blame he had carried for so long. He recognized that he was a child, a victim, and that he couldn't be held responsible for the actions of his abusers. He acknowledged the courage and resilience he had demonstrated in surviving those harrowing years, a resilience that he had initially overlooked amidst the overwhelming trauma. He began to see himself not as a victim defined by his past, but as a survivor empowered by his experiences.

The journey towards forgiveness of his mother and her boyfriend was even more complex. The rage, the bitterness, the desire for retribution – these emotions had been a constant companion for years. Dr. Albright helped him understand that these feelings were natural, understandable responses to the trauma he had endured. However, she also helped him see that holding onto these emotions would only perpetuate his suffering. She encouraged him to explore the complexities of their actions, to try to understand, not excuse, their behavior.

He began by researching the psychology of child abuse, delving into the factors that could contribute to such horrific acts. He learned about the cycle of abuse, the intergenerational trauma that could lead to repeated patterns of neglect and violence. He learned about the impact of poverty, addiction, and mental illness on family dynamics. He didn't condone their actions, but he began to understand, to a certain extent, the circumstances that may have contributed to their behavior. This wasn't an easy process. It required a profound act of empathy, a willingness to step outside his own pain and consider the perspectives of others, even those who had inflicted such profound suffering upon him.

He recognized that understanding wasn't the same as excusing or justifying their actions. He wasn't minimizing the severity of his ordeal, nor was he lessening the responsibility they bore for their crimes. Instead, he was acknowledging the complexity of human behavior, the interplay of factors that could contribute to both good and evil, and his own capacity for forgiveness, a capacity that was both remarkable and essential to his healing.

This process of forgiveness was interwoven with self-acceptance, a journey of recognizing his inherent worth and value, regardless of the trauma he had endured. He began to embrace his scars, both visible and invisible, as testament to his strength, his resilience, and his indomitable spirit. He started to recognize that his past didn't define him; it shaped him, but it didn't dictate his future. He learned to accept the parts of himself that he had previously rejected, the vulnerabilities, the insecurities, the lingering fears.

He began to cultivate self-compassion, treating himself with the kindness and understanding he would offer a close friend facing similar challenges. He practiced self-care, prioritizing his physical and mental well-being. He engaged in activities that brought him joy and peace, such as hiking, painting, and playing music. He reconnected with old friends and family members who supported his journey, cherishing the relationships that had weathered the storms of his ordeal. He made new connections with other survivors and advocates, finding solace and strength in shared experience.

This new chapter wasn't about erasing the past; it was about integrating it into a more holistic narrative of his life. It was about accepting the totality of his being, the good and the bad, the light and the shadow. It was about finding peace not in forgetting, but in remembering, in acknowledging his pain and celebrating his triumph over adversity. He understood that he would carry the scars of his past, but he would no longer be defined by them. He would carry them with dignity, with pride, as reminders of his unwavering strength, his resilience, and his capacity for both profound suffering and profound healing. His journey had taken him to the darkest of places, but it had also led him to a place of profound self-acceptance, forgiveness, and inner peace. He was finally free. He had not only survived; he had emerged stronger, wiser, and more compassionate than he could have ever imagined. The boy trapped in the attic was gone, replaced by a man who carried the torch of hope for countless others, a man who embodied the indomitable spirit of the human heart. His story served as a powerful testament to the transformative power of forgiveness, self-compassion, and the extraordinary capacity for healing inherent in the human spirit.

The crisp morning air bit at Joshua's cheeks as he stepped onto the porch of his cabin, the rising sun painting the snow-covered landscape in hues of gold and rose. He inhaled deeply, the scent of pine and damp earth filling his lungs, a familiar comfort that grounded him in the present moment. The solitude of the woods, once a refuge from the relentless demands of his advocacy work, now felt like a foundation, a place where he could nurture the fragile seedling of his new life.

The past eight months had been a whirlwind. The media frenzy surrounding his case had gradually subsided, replaced by a quieter, more sustained interest in his story. He had given a few carefully chosen interviews, his words carefully crafted to inspire hope and raise awareness about the systemic failures that allowed his abuse to happen for so long. He'd established a foundation dedicated to supporting child abuse survivors, a testament to his commitment to preventing similar tragedies from occurring. But he knew, deep down, that his true healing wasn't just about advocacy; it was about building a life that reflected the peace he was painstakingly constructing within himself.

His days were filled with a rhythm he had meticulously crafted – a blend of work and self-care. He rose early, exercising amidst the stillness of the forest, his body growing stronger, reflecting the increasing strength of his spirit. He spent hours in his small studio, painting, his canvases becoming vessels for his emotions, his brushstrokes expressing the turmoil and the tranquility that warred within him. The colors, once muted and somber, were now infused with a vibrancy he hadn't realized he possessed. He'd found a new outlet for his artistic talents, his paintings gaining recognition, slowly building a new identity for himself beyond the trauma. He even found himself selling pieces, the income providing a welcome supplement to his foundation's funding and allowing for further work to be done.

He started taking up carpentry as well, working with wood to create functional and beautiful pieces that filled his cabin with warmth and a sense of accomplishment. The rough texture of the wood felt reassuring against his hands, a grounding presence that contrasted with the often-abstract and overwhelming nature of his emotions. Each carefully crafted piece was a testament to his patience, his commitment to his own personal growth, the very resilience that had carried him through the darkest periods of his life.

His relationship with Dr. Albright continued, albeit at a less intense pace. Their sessions were now less focused on processing the past and more about navigating the complexities of building a fulfilling future. He discussed his fears about intimacy, the lingering anxieties about relationships, his apprehension about connecting with others on a deeper level. Dr. Albright had patiently helped him confront these issues, teaching him to recognize his own self-worth, and equipping him with the tools to navigate the challenges of forming healthy connections. The focus shifted from survival to thriving, from mending broken pieces to crafting a life he deserved.

He had made a few tentative steps towards forming new relationships, forging connections with other survivors who understood the invisible wounds he carried. He found comfort and strength in their shared experiences, discovering that his pain wasn't unique, but a shared burden of many, a connection that provided a sense of community and belonging he had lacked for so long. These relationships were carefully cultivated, a testament to his newfound awareness of healthy boundaries, a contrast to the coercive and manipulative relationships he experienced in his past.

He still visited his family periodically. The process was fraught with difficulties and a rollercoaster of emotions, from hope and optimism to disappointment and fear. However, he had learned to compartmentalize, to approach each visit with a measured resolve, and he was able to engage with family in his own terms, on his own timeline. His mother, while remorseful, struggled to understand the depths of the harm she had caused, still struggling with her own demons. Yet, through it all, a path towards a healthier relationship with his mother began to emerge, a path of acceptance, forgiveness and healing that was only possible through his own strength and unwavering self-compassion.

He had found an unexpected joy in acts of kindness, his own experiences compelling him to extend compassion to others in need. He volunteered at a local soup kitchen, finding purpose and fulfillment in serving those less fortunate. He spoke openly at schools and community centers, sharing his story not as a means of seeking pity, but as a beacon of hope, inspiring others to embrace their own resilience. The act of giving back, of helping others, filled him with a sense of purpose that transcended his personal journey, giving his healing a deeper and more meaningful dimension.

The scars remained, both visible and invisible. The physical reminders of his past were a constant presence, but they no longer held the power to define him. He had learned to see them not as symbols of shame but as testaments to his incredible survival. The psychological scars – the anxieties, the fears, the lingering trauma – were more insidious, but he had developed coping mechanisms, tools that empowered him to manage his emotions, navigate challenges, and build a life where he was the architect of his own happiness.

He learned to appreciate the small joys – the warmth of the sun on his skin, the quiet rustle of leaves in the wind, the simple pleasure of a cup of coffee in the morning. He found beauty in the ordinary, a stark contrast to the monotonous and oppressive reality of his past. He appreciated the subtle rhythms of life, valuing each day as a precious gift, an opportunity to live fully, to experience the richness and wonder of his existence.

He had found love, a quiet, tender connection with a woman who understood his past but didn't define him by it. She loved him not for his story, but for the man he had become – strong, resilient, compassionate, and deeply loving. Their relationship was a testament to his capacity for vulnerability and connection, a triumph of healing over trauma. It was a partnership built on trust, respect, and a shared desire to create a life filled with joy, laughter, and unconditional love. Their love was a refuge from his past, a beacon guiding him towards his future. It wasn't a replacement for the love he missed, but an addition, a flourishing relationship

built on a foundation of self-love
and acceptance.

He still struggled at times,
experiencing moments of despair,
flashbacks, nightmares. But he had
learned to navigate these difficulties,
equipped with the tools of self-
compassion and resilience. He
understood that healing wasn't a
linear process, a destination but a
continuous journey, marked by
highs and lows, breakthroughs and
setbacks. His resilience was not only
a survival trait but had become his
cornerstone, his strength. And so, he
continued his journey, ever moving
forward, his gaze fixed on a future
forged in resilience and hope. He
was a testament to the indomitable
spirit of the human heart, his life a
living embodiment of the
transformative power of healing,
forgiveness, and the unshakeable
strength found within the depths of

human experience. He was Joshua, and his story was one of survival, but more importantly, a story of triumphant resilience.

Dedication

This book would not have been possible without the unwavering support and guidance of many individuals. Dredging up old memories and reliving stories through writing can sometimes take a toll on your mental wellness, but the reward is worth it.

Glossary

This glossary defines key terms used throughout the book related to child abuse, trauma, and the legal system:

Child Abuse: The physical, sexual, or emotional maltreatment or neglect of a child.

Neglect: The failure to provide a child with adequate care, supervision, or necessities.

Trauma: A deeply distressing or disturbing experience.

PTSD (Post-Traumatic Stress Disorder): A mental health condition triggered by a terrifying event.

Foster Care: A system of care for children who cannot live with their families.

CPS (Child Protective Services):
Government agencies responsible
for investigating reports of child
abuse and neglect.

Author

A. Abney was raised in New England and is the author of several crime and drama books. He draws from his background in law enforcement and psychology to create griping tales that captivates his readers. He also authored his memoir, Divided "A Memoir of a Family I Never Knew", which details his journey through DNA to find his biological family.